"My destiny
doesn't rest here."

Victoria said it quietly as Damien swung the car
through the big iron gates that had been there
since their great-great-grandfathers had built the
mills.

"It rests with me," Damien said softly, "and there's
nothing to be afraid of, Victoria. It is only the same
destiny you ran away from six years ago. It has to
be," he added simply.

It sounded like a trap closing around her. If Damien
believed all this about the mills, wasn't he trapped,
too? Perhaps he didn't really want to marry her.

"We don't have to be tied into this, Damien," she
said softly.

"Then perhaps we should never have been born.
As we were born, we are tied into it. In any case,"
he added evenly, "it's not all business. I want
you, Victoria."

Patricia Wilson used to live in Yorkshire, England, but with her children all grown up, she decided to give up her teaching position there and accompany her husband on an extended trip to Spain. Their travels are providing her with plenty of inspiration for her romance writing.

Books by Patricia Wilson

BOND
OF DESTINY

Patricia Wilson

Harlequin Books

TORONTO • NEW YORK • LONDON
AMSTERDAM • PARIS • SYDNEY • HAMBURG
STOCKHOLM • ATHENS • TOKYO • MILAN

Original hardcover edition published in 1989
by Mills & Boon Limited

ISBN 0-373-03102-5

Harlequin Romance first edition January 1991

CHAPTER ONE

'YOU should see the man who's just walked in!'

Victoria didn't know the name of the model who was speaking, and she gave only a faint smile. She wasn't interested. Once this day was over, she would be back to her flat and a good sleep. She felt as if she needed a whole week of sleep. This was the third fashion show in a fortnight, and her normal photographic sessions had to be fitted in somehow. Work was coming thick and fast these days, ever since she had become cover girl for three magazines in a row. She wanted the work, the independence it gave, but it would have been nice to get some sleep. Her agent was pushing work at her too fast. Some days she had been almost double-booked, having to race across London by taxi to make the next appointment in time.

'Victoria! The midnight blue chiffon is next.'

Madame Gautier stepped in through the curtains and frowned, her face lightening as she saw that Victoria was ready.

'Perfect!' Her throaty whisper was all approval. 'It is the most expensive dress of the collection, and you wear it beautifully.' Her eyes ran over Victoria's slender height, her pale blonde hair that fell like silk over her shoulders, her creamy skin and the changing green of her eyes. 'So cold. So perfect. Just what the dress needs. It is a midnight sky against cold moonlight.'

She flashed a brittle smile, satisfied with her own poetical fancy, and stepped back to the salon.

'Victoria in Midnight Intrigue!' she announced, deliberately thickening her French accent, and Victoria stepped forward.

'Look to the back. The man!'

The frantic whisper almost made Victoria smile, and that would never do—not in Midnight Intrigue! She stepped through the curtains and out on to the raised catwalk: cool, sure of herself, and faintly amused.

This was an exclusive show for the very rich. Only the very rich could afford the clothes. Only the very rich were invited. She walked forward slowly, the soft music adding to the expensive atmosphere of the long salon, with its gilt chairs and glittering mirrors, its flowers on pedestals a perfect setting for both the clothes that were on show and those worn by the clients.

The salon was full, every seat taken, and Victoria's green eyes scanned the clientele coolly. There was a murmur of approval that rippled around the salon, the sound as soft as the exclusive smell of mingled perfumes. The women were either wealthy, or had wealthy escorts. There were few of them here who would be unable to afford Midnight Intrigue—and few of them who would be able to get into it! This was not the sort of work she enjoyed. The studio work was harder, but at least it was private.

She stopped at the end of the catwalk and slowly turned, pausing to give them time to see the dress from every angle. Almost every movement was timed in her head. She knew exactly how long to stand, how to move subtly to the most interested viewer. She allowed her eyes to focus, and then she saw the man standing at the back of the room and her heart almost stopped.

Damien!

The tall, hard, masculine body was the same. The same black hair framed his handsome head. The eyes, as blue as forget-me-nots, were icily cold, and she froze to the spot.

For seconds his eyes held hers and there was no expression on his face at all. He was a cold, accusing stranger, his power holding her still, until an intrigued murmur from the wealthy clientele warned her that she was not moving, that she was the focus of all eyes, that there were others in this room besides herself and Damien Hunt.

She turned and walked back, steeling herself for the final turn at the end, drifting through the curtains when she would have liked to run.

'What is wrong? You held the pause at the end for far too long! You are ill?'

Madame Gautier's voice was more accusing than concerned, and Victoria hurried to change, barely noticing her.

'I'm quite all right, *madame*,' she said hurriedly. 'I have to go now. You're quite finished with me, I believe?'

'Well, yes. But it is usual for the models to stay. There may be a client who would like another showing of the dress.'

'I'm sorry.' Victoria faced the disapproval squarely. It was easier than staying to face Damien. What was he doing here? Who had he brought?

He was wealthy enough to buy any or all of the dresses for some woman. The thought brought a sick feeling to the pit of her stomach, and she began to change to her street clothes determinedly.

'My assignments are running very late today,' she said firmly. 'I'm afraid some other model will have to show the dress if anyone wants a further look.'

'The dress was supposed to be in *Discretion* next month,' Madame Gautier reminded her in a threatening voice.

'And as you know, I've already modelled it for the photographs. I imagine that the magazine is made-up by now. They work quite far ahead. Still, if you want it done by another model——'

'No, no! You are at the top of your career. On you, the dress is perfection!'

Two can threaten, Victoria thought grimly. The sight of a bully backing off would have amused her, but with Damien Hunt out there nothing was amusing. She wanted to be miles from here before the champagne was handed round. Even if he had come for a glimpse of her, which was unlikely, he would not expect her to just disappear. He had no idea now where she lived.

She slipped into her clothes—a deep blue woollen dress and knee-high beige boots—and after one quick flick to her long hair she picked up her things and made her way out of the building by the back door. Even so, she had to go round the front because this was a cul-de-sac, and the first thing she saw was Dale's car.

'Hurry up, darling!' He stuck his head out of the window and called to her. 'I've already been warned about parking here. If the traffic warden comes back this way I'll get a ticket.'

Relief washed over her. Dale West was the most obliging of photographers. He knew she was really hard pressed today. Nobody else would have left the studio to make sure his model made it on time for a session.

'Oh, Dale, you're a real peach! I had to make a run for it as it was. I'll be on time now.'

She saw Dale's expression change from self-satisfaction to utter astonishment, and then her arm was taken in a vice-like grip that told her only too well who was standing behind her.

'You're not going anywhere, Victoria!' Damien's voice was like ice, and anger mixed with outright panic as Victoria swung to face him.

'What are *you* doing here?'

It was only because she had seen him in the salon that Victoria managed to control her voice to match the coldness of his—to return a measure of the arrogance.

'I've come for *you*.' There was utter condemnation in his voice as he added, 'Your grandfather died late last night.'

She just stared at him, waiting for him to tell her it wasn't true, that it was just another cruelty, but he said nothing. Only the blue of his eyes held her to reality, her own eyes, green and filled with pain, locked with his. She moved her arm from his grasp, her lashes slowly lowering and, as if a sustaining power had left her, the world began to spin madly.

'Victoria!'

She heard Dale's voice, warning and anxious, but he was not in time. It was Damien who caught her, the feel of his arms after so long an added shock that drove her further. She blacked out.

'Did you have to tell her like that? Couldn't you have been gentle?'

Dale's tone was angry as she began to recover after only a second and Damien's deep, quiet reply chilled her.

'A truth is a truth, no matter how it's told. She knows now, and I'll take it from there.'

Truth! Truth was a thing for other people. Damien did as he wished. Victoria shuddered, controlling her voice with difficulty.

'Thank you. I'm quite all right now.'

She opened her eyes, and almost closed them again in an act of sheer self-defence. She was still cradled against Damien's chest as he held her effortlessly in his arms, and she struggled for composure, drawn to look at him even against her will, her gaze once again locked with his. His eyes were so blue—richly, perfectly blue, the dark ring around the iris making them more brilliant still, the lashes as raven-black as his hair.

His face was without expression, the only movement from his eyes as they left hers to roam over her face, noting the growing pallor. She closed her eyes abruptly to shut out the hard good looks, the firm, carved lips.

'You can put me down thank you.' She managed it with no tremor whatsoever, and he allowed her to stand, his arm still supporting her until she turned sharply away to face Dale.

'I'll have to go, Dale. I'm letting you down, but——'

'Not to worry, darling,' he said softly. 'I'll get someone else, and anything that can will wait until you get back. Just take it easy, right?'

'I'll have to go back to my flat, and then I'll get the next train out,' Victoria began. 'I—I'll let you know when...'

Her hands anxiously smoothed her hair behind her ears, a little habit she had never lost from childhood— always a sign of anxiety; Damien's eyes narrowed at this trembling little slip as she quickly snatched her hands away and clasped them tightly.

'You're coming with me,' he asserted coolly, bending to collect her things before she could move. 'I'll take you to your flat, and then we'll get off. I want to be back up north before dark.'

She was stunned by this arrogant assumption that she would do exactly as she was told, although she should not have been at all surprised—after all, she knew him well enough—hadn't he been like this all her life? It had been a long time ago, though. He was about to find out that she was no longer at all malleable. Her life was her own now.

'I should go with him if I were you,' Dale advised softly, as Damien strode to his car. 'You're in no fit state to travel alone. Does he always act like this—whoever he is?'

'For as long as I can remember,' Victoria said wearily, and she could remember far too much at this moment.

Her eyes followed Damien as he unlocked a Ferrari. It was shining, sleek, red—and he had a parking ticket too. He simply tore it free and pushed it into his pocket. Things like that never disturbed him. *Nothing* disturbed him. Damien had always known exactly where he was going and who was going with him!

'Ring me, darling!'

Dale gave her a quick peck on the cheek, and drove off, after one quick look at Damien's impatient face. Victoria walked to the car, trying to ignore the firm, hard hand that helped her.

'The boyfriend, or one of many?' Damien asked sardonically as he pulled out into the traffic.

'He's a photographer. I work with him quite a lot.'

'Darling?' he enquired sharply. 'Does he normally call you that?'

'More often than not. It doesn't mean a lot here.' Victoria forced herself to be calm. There was no way that she was going to be drawn into any argument. She had always lost, and this time she didn't intend to even begin.

'A beautiful word ruined,' he derided. 'When someone says it to you and really means it, you'll wonder what hit you.'

'I usually know what hit me,' Victoria murmured drily. 'Normally, it's you.'

'Not for six long years,' he reminded her softly. 'Now things are different, princess.'

'Don't call me that!' She rounded on him with flashing eyes, her resolve to stay calm forgotten, and his gaze skimmed her face.

'At least it brought some animation.' There was grim satisfaction in his voice, and his eyes went back to the traffic. 'With Andrew gone, there'll be a great change— or didn't you expect an old man to die?' he murmured. 'Did you imagine you could run out on him for six years, never get in touch in all that time, and then come back to collect your dues like a good little girl?'

She opened her mouth to tell him that she *had* seen her grandfather, that they had written to each other regularly, that twice a year he had been down to London to stay with her, but it was none of Damien's business. Let him think what he liked. He could taunt as much as he wanted. It was nothing new.

Evidently her grandfather had kept his word, and told Damien nothing. The thought of him softened her cold expression, brought a smile to her lips and, though it was a very small smile, Damien saw it.

'Things are different!' he snapped. 'Smiles are out of order. Be advised, Victoria, and don't count any chickens.'

'I learned not to do that a long time ago,' she said coldly, memory wiping the smile away and twisting her heart. 'I realise that things will be different. Presumably you realise that too, as it's going to affect you?'

'And what could you do that would affect me?' he mocked.

'I now own half of the firm. You probably realise that I'm going to sell out.' She said it with as much venom as she could muster, hurt and memory clouding her voice, and he laughed, a low, grating sound.

'Don't say anything you may regret, my lady,' he warned coldly. 'Only the person with the whip can crack it. Wait and see!'

Victoria stood at the graveside and watched her grandfather being buried. The last of a line of Kendals. No other man would now bear that name. Her own name would change when she married—*if* she married.

The wind blew the skirt of her black suit, moulding it to her slender hips. The pale, shining blonde hair blew back from her delicately beautiful face, the changing green of her eyes darkened as she looked across the valley at the brilliant neon lights that would soon take on a new meaning.

Kendal and Hunt Mills. The words were etched in red across the sky, as they had been for the whole of her life, proudly and defiantly proclaiming the names of the two families who had brought work and stability to this valley for generations. Two families inextricably entwined in friendship and duty. The last Kendal was gone, except for her, and she suddenly felt inadequate, incapable of carrying the burden of duty, even if she had intended to do so.

She had thought her grandfather indestructible, her mind forcefully pushing aside the reality that one day he would no longer be here to bully her, protect her, make plans that she had always fought against vigorously. Now he would never plan again. She shivered in the cold wind. Why were funerals so cold, so lonely? Her jacket was not thick enough, she told herself; the shivering was simply because of the cold—not the aching fear the loss of Andrew Kendal had left with her.

Joel tightened his hand on hers, comforting and dependable, his position at her side almost angrily protective. Where else would he be but here, standing beside her? And where else would Damien be, but grimly guarding her other side? They were heirs too, the other half of a legend, but there was no anxiety in Damien Hunt—he ruled everything and everyone. He ruled the mills, he ruled his brother Joel, but he would never rule her!

No doubt he was standing here planning, just as her grandfather had always planned, his plans as often as not made with Damien. What power was to be in those long-fingered, capable hands now? She realised how very much alone she was, even though Joel was her friend. He would be exactly what his brother allowed him to be. Damien's hold on *her* was utterly broken, though. She would leave this valley and never return.

She sighed, a small sound of misery and protest, the chains of duty a weight that tried to hold her to the ground, like a ghost that protested at her decision to sell out and wipe the Kendal name from the sky, and Damien's hand came to her shoulder.

It was not a comfort. It was a reminder. There were people here, neighbours from the valley, workmen from the mills. She was a Kendal! Damien's hand said it all, and she straightened her slim shoulders, shrugging him away, anger warming her in the cold air. Joel had always been like a brother, he was close to her own age, but Damien had been as he was now: powerful, arrogant, domineering—and he had always despised her. He had despised her enough to imagine that she was a fool.

They drove back to the great house on the hill, Damien and Joel still with her, both silent, but for entirely different reasons. Joel was hurting for her; Damien was thinking. She watched the house as they approached— watched it as she had never watched it before. It was hers now, this great Victorian structure built by her great-great-grandfather to display his wealth and his grip on the valley. There was another house on the opposite hillside, and she always thought of it as Damien's house, although it was as much Joel's, and Damien was rarely there.

Molly was waiting as usual, her eyes anxiously on Victoria's face. She was serving very small amounts of sherry, and Victoria noted the fact with some amusement.

Molly's concern was for Victoria, as it had always been since she had come here to keep house for Andrew Kendal, when his son and daughter-in-law had died leaving him with a four-year-old grandchild to rear.

'You need rest,' Molly sidled up to her and spoke grimly. 'Why these people are here, I don't know!'

'It's usual, Molly,' Victoria said quietly. 'They expect it.'

'Well, walk round and have a word, and then let's get them on their way,' Molly grunted, her face as bleak as the moorland in winter. 'I'm thinking of you—they can expect what they like!'

It seemed wise to obey. Molly hovered over the sherry in a truly menacing way. It was not going to be long before even the most resolute became aware that, as far as far as this forbidding woman was concerned, they were not welcome. Molly's smile to Damien, though, was deferential—wasn't everyone's smile deferential to Damien?

She had taken charge of Victoria when Damien had brought her home two days ago. They had all wanted her to stay with Damien and Joel, but she had refused flatly, preferring the loneliness of the big house to being close to Damien, and Molly had mothered her. There was nothing to do. Of course Damien had done everything.

Jeremy Lloyd was there, representing his family. She had almost forgotten him, and he came up to her, murmuring his regrets, his eyes telling her something entirely different. He had always been interested, as much as he dared be with Damien around, but now she was so clearly her own master, no longer a bewildered girl, and of course she was rich. It might have been an unkind thought, but she was no longer very gullible—experience had cured her of that fault.

'Molly's making everyone feel unwelcome,' he murmured, not entirely in amusement.

'I think that's her intention,' Victoria told him wearily. She was tired, suffering the aftermath of shock, and she was glad when Joel rejoined her. 'She wants me to rest.'

'Molly has no idea of the right thing to do,' Jeremy said in amazement. 'She probably thinks that you're still a child. She's always had a lot of authority here.' His tone implied he knew she no longer would have, but Victoria was too weary to argue, even on Molly's side.

'Go and tell her if she's offending you,' Joel advised him shortly. 'She'll probably box your ears, but you never know your luck!'

He didn't take the advice, Victoria noticed. Molly in her present mood was a little daunting, and soon people began to drift away until only Jeremy and Joel were left.

'I'll ring you tomorrow, Victoria,' Jeremy assured her in a softened tone, Molly's eyes being firmly on him. 'I'll be round to see you.'

'What role does he imagine he's going to have in your life?' Joel asked, as they watched Jeremy leave. 'Don't encourage him, Vic. He's so damned righteous! Don't marry him, will you, love? I couldn't stand it, and Damien would have to alter the mill sign. Lloyd and Hunt! It doesn't have a good ring.'

'Jeremy's harmless, I imagine,' Victoria said tiredly. 'In any case, I'll be leaving. I live and work in London.'

'What does Damien say?' Joel murmured a trifle anxiously, and for a moment she even felt angry with Joel. The obsession that everyone had always had with what Damien Hunt thought was no longer part of her life. He was no longer a giant in her mind.

'Damien has nothing at all to do with me. He's your problem, Joel. He's not *my* brother!'

'No,' he said softly, his eyes quickly scanning her beautiful, cool face at the sharp sound of her voice. 'He's not somebody you can just ignore though, Vic.'

She smiled frostily, but said nothing. Watch me, she thought grimly!

As Joel left, Victoria began to follow Molly up the stairs, as obedient now in her grief as she had been at four years old, when Molly had taken the reins of this house firmly into her capable hands, but the sight of Damien in her grandfather's study brought her to a startled and annoyed halt. Molly disappeared as she saw Damien's tight face.

'I thought you'd gone,' Victoria said coldly, walking in to confront him. 'What can I do for you?'

'Not a lot.' He turned to look at her as she stood just inside the door. 'I want to talk to you, but not today when you're so upset. However, it would be a good idea if we were to have a quiet word with each other before the will is read tomorrow.'

'I can't see why.' Victoria watched him warily, totally on guard, her weariness forgotten. It had always been wise to be wary with Damien Hunt, and she had realised that even when she was only a child.

She had been accustomed to going in and out of the house on the opposite hill as if it were a second home. Kenneth and Audrey Hunt had spoiled her, and Joel had been her friend and playmate. Damien had rarely been there. He was too grown up to be noticed. He was at university when she was small and first allowed to cross to the Hunts' house, and later he had been away a lot, although she hadn't realised then exactly why.

She had never let him worry her, until she discovered with childlike hurt that he disliked her. She was twelve when he finally came home from university and began to take up his responsibility in the mills, and apparently her constant presence at his home annoyed him, although he adored his younger brother. It had taken years for that hurt to die.

He had walked into the drawing-room for a second as she was sitting waiting for Joel, and he had merely raised dark eyebrows, his cool blue eyes unsmiling. She heard his voice in the hall as he walked out again and encountered his mother.

'I see that the beautiful brat is here again,' he remarked, apparently thinking that all twelve-year-old girls were deaf. 'Maybe we should adopt her and install her here permanently?'

Victoria never heard Audrey Hunt's reply. Her eyes filled with tears at the cold sarcasm, and she shot out of the house via the french windows, running home as fast as her legs would go. Thereafter Joel had been obliged to visit *her*, although he was a bit scared of her grandfather.

She became aware that Damien was standing by her grandfather's desk, his eyes cold and blue as he looked back at her impatiently.

'If you've come out of your trance,' he said drily, 'I'll tell you why! When the will is read, you'll find that life is to be a little different from your expectations. Things are not about to be as you imagine.'

'As you haven't the faintest idea what I imagine,' Victoria said sharply, quelling the sudden drumming of her heart, 'I fail to see how you've come to that conclusion. In any case, you don't know what the will says.'

'As a matter of fact, I know exactly what the will says,' Damien assured her softly, coming forward to tower over her. 'Don't forget that your grandfather and I have been partners since my father died. We conferred constantly.'

'Plotted!' Victoria corrected coldly.

'No.' His voice was indifferent, her opinion not interesting him at all. 'I valued your grandfather's advice normally, even though he left things mainly to me these past few years. Naturally I knew what was in his mind about most subjects. Therefore, I know what's in the will.'

'So tell me now.'

Victoria moved away from him. He always made her feel useless. There was always this feeling that he wanted her to be completely dependent on him. Well, she had foiled his plans for taking over everything. She had done that a long time ago.

'I have no intention of telling you now, when you're so uptight and—hostile!' he snapped, apparently annoyed that she didn't break down and beg him to take over her life. 'I'll see you tomorrow morning and we'll talk then. Meanwhile, get to bed and rest. I heard Molly telling you to do just that. She's a woman with a great deal of sense.'

'So am I!' Victoria informed him angrily.

'Are you?' He walked over and tilted her flushed face. 'You were twenty-four a few months ago. I imagine legally that makes you a woman, but *life* makes people into adults, and you've never had to face life.'

'You imagine I'm still a brat, then?' she snapped unwisely, her face reddening at his amused surprise.

'Possibly,' he murmured. 'A very beautiful brat, though. Even more beautiful now—and no doubt just as unreliable and selfish.'

He had the insolence to stroke her hair back from her face and fix it behind her ears, reminding her of her childhood habit. His lips quirked with amusement at her gasp of outrage, and she was really glad that Molly came back at that moment with 'no more nonsense' clearly written across her grim face.

Damien walked out, smiling in his normal superior manner, and Victoria was only too glad to follow Molly upstairs.

'I put your electric blanket on,' Molly said quietly, urging Victoria into her large, well-lit bedroom.

'It's not cold,' Victoria said vaguely, undressing mechanically, her eyes seeing nothing at all.

'You'll relax,' Molly informed her in a determined voice. 'I'll get you up when it's time for dinner.'

'Don't bother.'

She slid into bed and Molly never answered—she was already leaving the bedroom, and Victoria knew that she would do as she thought fit, whatever was best in her opinion. Right now, Molly could get away with anything. There was no fight in Victoria at all. Maybe tomorrow...

She dreamed of Damien, and awoke with a start, as dusk was settling on the landscape. It was not unusual to dream of him, but this time she had been back in time, back to the golden days when she had begun to be grown-up, her life secure with her grandfather.

She fought to hold the dream, her eyes wide in the semi-darkness of the room, as she saw again the streets of the town, the road leading to her own house...

She was fifteen, home from boarding school, trying to pick up some thread of her past. Her wealthy grandfather, her private school, had distanced her from everyone, but she was discovering that she was at least popular with the boys in town. She was on her bicycle, stopped at the edge of the road, talking to two of them, laughing and happy, seeing the admiration in their eyes, and Damien drove past, his car screaming to a halt as he saw her.

He made her feel guilty, as if she was doing something horribly wrong, and she was red with shame when he got out and ordered her home.

'I'm on my way there!' she said angrily, as the two boys mounted their cycles with unseemly haste and departed. 'It's not up to you to order me about!'

'As your grandfather is not here to see you, I'm standing in for him,' Damien said tightly. 'You either ride home now, or I put you in the car and throw that machine in the back!'

'I'm nothing to do with you!' Victoria raged. 'You can't bully me even though you bully Joel. I'm not your sister.'

'A fact that gives me endless hours of satisfaction,' he bit out. 'I do not bully Joel, because he never needs to be told how to behave.'

'I've done nothing wrong at all!' Victoria protested violently.

'Your name is Kendal!' Damien snapped furiously. 'Remember that. Next time you decide to flirt with the local boys, understand that your grandfather would not be pleased.'

His eyes moved over her slim figure, clad in shorts and shirt, and it made her feel more guilty than ever, but she couldn't let him get away with it.

'I'm no more important than the girls in town,' she said bitterly. 'Joel sees whoever he likes, and I'm no different. Everyone knows you and talks to you, even though you *are* King of the Castle!'

Momentarily his mouth quirked with laughter—but only momentarily.

'You're a girl,' Damien said sternly. 'That makes you different.'

'The town's full of girls,' Victoria seethed. 'Go and order them about!'

'I have no desire to do any such thing,' Damien said impatiently, obviously annoyed at this teenage defiance. '*You* are my concern for now.'

'Why?' she persisted. 'Why am I any special concern of yours?'

'You're cellophane-wrapped,' he taunted. 'Your grandfather has brought you up to be nicely and deli-

cately packaged. We must see that you stay just like that.
Now please go home before I get annoyed.'

She went, but she was fuming, and she noticed later
in the holidays that, when he saw her in town shopping
with a boy walking beside her, he ignored her as usual.
Of course, she wasn't wearing shorts then, but she wondered darkly if he had simply been in a mood before,
and had stopped to take it out on her. It seemed likely.
She complained bitterly to her grandfather, but he
laughed uproariously, and she got no sense out of him
at all...

She got out of bed and went to the window, looking
across the valley. She could see lights on in the huge
stone house on the opposite hillside. Damien was there,
and her much-loved Joel—but it was Damien who would
be trying to plan her life. He could think again. She had
hated him for years!

CHAPTER TWO

JOEL phoned the next day, and offered to take her out for a while to look around the place, but one of his remarks almost put her off going.

'By the way, Vic,' he said with a sudden laugh. 'A snippet of information that may amuse you. Guess who Damien has as a secretary at the mill? Heather Lloyd! Remember her? Don't tell anyone I told you this, but I think that they're pretty cosy—at least, she behaves as if she's a little more than a secretary. I wouldn't be surprised if all her efforts finally paid off!'

Victoria agreed reluctantly to an outing. Anything to enable her to put the phone down. It seemed that everything now was bringing back memories she had squashed for a long time, and Heather Lloyd was one of them.

There had been a time when she had been friendly with Jeremy's sister, in an uneasy sort of way. They had gone to the same school, and Heather had vigorously maintained their friendship, although she was an entirely different character from Victoria. Her father was a stockbroker, spending most of his time in London and coming up to the big house in town only often enough to lay down rules of behaviour, and impress upon Jeremy the rightness of things.

As far as Heather was concerned, it did little good. Right was anything she could get away with, and even at seventeen she had moved from one scrape to another, her escapades covered rapidly by either Jeremy or his mother. Victoria's grandfather had not been impressed by their cosmopolitan ways, and discouraged any friendship—an oblique order that had made a very good reason for Victoria to continue it, but she was always a little uneasy...

She went to Heather's seventeenth birthday party, feeling more anxious than usual when she discovered that Joel had turned down his invitation. Damien had been invited too. That had stunned her a little. Damien was twenty-seven and not into children's parties, a fact he had impressed on her mockingly when she had invited him to her own party a few weeks previously. Naturally, *he* wasn't going either and, as Joel drove her there, she wished she had also refused. Even Joel seemed to be disapproving, at one with Damien in this.

She was soon more uneasy than ever. The party was not at all like her own. Only Heather and herself were teenagers. The other guests were in their late-twenties and early-thirties. With Mr Lloyd Senior in London, as usual, there seemed to be nobody there to keep an eye on anything. Her mother was merely weakly indulgent, and Heather behaved as she wished, the guests her own in spite of the age difference. It was certainly not a party for any innocent girl, and before too long Victoria's cheeks were red, escape the uppermost thing on her mind.

She had been inveigled into a corner by one ardent guest, his drink-laden breath hot against her embarrassed face, when she looked up and saw Damien. His black brows were drawn into an angry line above icily cold eyes. How long he had been there she didn't know, but her green eyes appealed to him, and he was in any case already moving into furious action.

Her partner reeled from Damien's flat hand against his chest, and Victoria was marched firmly out, Heather's face angry and disappointed as she watched them leave.

He drove off with some violence as Victoria sat in silence, too embarrassed to speak. Damien's anger was a tangible thing, filling the car, but as they approached her house she voiced her anxiety quickly.

'I can't go home yet,' she begged, a little desperately. 'I'll have to explain why I'm back so soon. Grandfather will be furious with me.'

'All right!' Damien grimly turned the car towards the dark, open moors. 'We'll drive for a while until you manage to slide back into your normal character.'

She wasn't quite sure what he meant, but coming from Damien it had to be something pretty awful.

'I—I don't know how long I was there...' she murmured anxiously after a while, his stony silence making things much worse.

'An hour!' he rasped. 'One hour too long.'

'I—I could have managed,' she began, her blonde head coming up defiantly. 'If you hadn't been there I would have——'

'Behaved like Heather Lloyd?' he finished for her harshly. 'Don't ever let me catch you at it!'

'I wouldn't!' Victoria gasped in a shocked voice, her defiance fading a little at the picture he painted with no subtlety. 'You're not my keeper anyway,' she added, in an attempt to steer off any further remarks of that kind. 'My grandfather tells me what to do.'

'He's not always capable, apparently,' Damien grated. 'You seem to be able to get away with most things, in spite of his loud threats. You're not quite what you seem, are you, Little Miss Kendal? I hope they keep a strict eye on you at that school for Andrew's sake! A few more hours at that party and you'd be quite at home, I imagine. At any time you're more impressed by the polish of the Lloyds than shocked by their behaviour.'

'You have no business to speak to me like that!' Victoria snapped angrily, colour flooding her face in the darkness. The party had terrified her, but, as usual, Damien thought the worst of her. 'Jeremy Lloyd behaves very well,' she added hotly, gulping down a sudden feeling of unhappiness. 'He's a perfect gentleman.'

'An older gentleman,' Damien corrected coolly. 'He's almost my age.'

'What does it matter?' She was suddenly worried for no reason at all.

'You're seventeen! Remember that when somebody else starts mauling you.'

'Nobody was—mauling me!'

'Somebody was all set to begin, but I got there a bit too soon. You didn't have the time to find out whether you liked it or not.'

He seemed to be speaking through clenched teeth, and she glanced at him a bit timidly. His face was tight and hard, and he was making her miserable.

'I wouldn't have liked it, Damien,' she assured him, a little tearfully. 'I'm glad you came, but there's no reason for you to speak so—so cruelly to me.'

He always made her feel she had done something wrong. Sometimes he made it so very obvious that he disliked her, and she never knew why.

'If you feel like facing your grandfather we'll go back,' he said quietly, some of the harshness dying from his voice, 'and I'm not cruel to you, Victoria. Heaven knows where I got the instinct from to come for you tonight! I seem to have a highly developed sense of protection as far as you're concerned. Maybe it's because you're the only girl in the two families. I feel that you're in danger from your so-called friends.'

'It's only Heather who's my friend, and I never do anything wrong,' she said miserably. She had felt quite grown-up tonight, before that dreadful party got under way. Now she just felt dominated and tearful.

He pulled quietly into her drive and stopped.

'I know deep down that you don't do anything wrong,' he conceded softly. 'It would show on your face. And she's not your friend, Victoria. She's light-years older, predatory by nature. She already sees you as a rival, and one day she'll try to take somebody who's yours.'

'How could she?' Victoria suddenly felt breathless, inordinately anxious. 'I only have my grandfather and Molly. If she took Molly she'd soon want to bring her back. Joel can't stand Heather,' she added quickly.

She got out of the car fast, her hair very pale in the moonlight. She felt fluttery inside. Normally she could get very angry with Damien, but tonight she wanted him to assure her that nothing had changed, even if he had to snap at her.

Back at the party she had seen Heather trying to interest him, the dress her mother had allowed her to wear shockingly slinky. Victoria had been horrified, and Damien had been tight-lipped and disapproving, but maybe he wasn't always like that. She had never thought of him as a man before. He was so godlike in all their eyes, and very alarming. Now he seemed to be dangerously close to her own life—not so safely distant.

The old path to the moors came to the edge of the garden, her own private little world. Joel had been allowed here to her favourite place when she was small, when she had lived in a world of make-believe, and she raced up the path now, searching for the old thoughts that suddenly seemed threatened. She had often sat up here and hated Damien.

'Victoria! You'll fall, you crazy girl. It's almost too dark to see,' Damien called to her urgently, but she wanted to get away, she didn't even want to hear his voice, and she went on climbing the path, her goal the black rock at the very top.

He came up too, reaching her as she sat stiffly on the rock, her face turned to the valley and the vividly written names of their families. He should have been angry— he usually was when she had been stupid, or even when she hadn't been—but he came quietly and stood laughing up at her as she sat on the rock, her long legs swinging.

Victoria didn't often get the chance to stare down at Damien. Normally he towered over her, but now she could look down, and she frowned at him because she couldn't think of anything else to do and because he was making her feel peculiar.

Even in the near darkness his eyes seemed to be blue. The lights from the mill reflected against his black hair, and her frowns faded until she was simply looking at him, puzzled as she had never been by her own odd feelings.

'Victoria's throne.' His voice was quietly amused. 'I remember when you first scrambled up here. You were about five, and you couldn't get down again. Joel came tearing home to raise the alarm, as your grandfather was out, and guess who had to rescue you?'

'I'm not five now,' Victoria said apprehensively, 'and I don't need rescuing.'

'Who rescued you tonight?' he queried softly. 'You would have been in a fix right now, wouldn't you?'

'No, I wouldn't. You can leave me here, Damien,' she said quickly. 'I can find my own way down.'

'And break a leg, for which I'll have to take the blame?' he taunted. 'Not likely, Your Highness! Down you come and in you go. Save all that dignity for your grandfather. You can be yourself with me.'

He took her by the waist and swung her down, and she felt a very different nervousness with him for the first time in her life, as he held her narrow waist and looked down at her.

'I always am myself. That's why you're always so—so angry with me. You don't have to pretend to be nice. We—we just don't like each other.'

His face was quite impossible to see, his head and powerful shoulders outlined against the red glow from the mills.

'Don't we?' His hands tightened slightly on her waist. 'Your grandfather lives very much in the past. He doesn't see what I see.'

'You mean he thinks I'm perfectly respectable, and you don't?' She glared up at him and saw his smile.

'I mean he sees no danger for you. I can't watch you all the time—some of us have to work. And if I thought you weren't—respectable, you'd be over my knee now for a good spanking, instead of talking quietly to me.'

'I don't need watching,' Victoria said tightly, even her skin feeling anxious. 'And I don't want to talk quietly to you. I want to go home.'

'Of course,' he agreed, with a laugh that worried her. 'Isn't that where you're going now?'

She turned to walk off, but he reached for her hand, preventing her from falling headlong. She tried to pull away and failed—his hand merely tightened and he delivered her to her door in a state little better than the one she had been in as she had left the party. Her heart was fluttering madly, and she had no idea why—except that, as usual, Damien had tied her into knots, and she felt he had been laughing at her. She hated it when he laughed at her.

After that, though, his attitude to her changed, as if that night was some kind of catalyst. The blue eyes no longer looked at her coldly and accusingly. He seemed to be trying hard to be nice to her. Her ways no longer seemed to annoy him, and if he walked in when she was in the middle of a battle with her grandfather, it was usually Andrew Kendal who was at the receiving end of Damien's icy stare. Suddenly his habit of coming into the house when he felt like it was a comfort.

Heather still persisted with her friendship and, as her school life had cut her off from most other people in the district, Victoria did not discourage her, although she didn't like the way Heather's eyes followed Damien. Damien was different, not like other people, and he was not a boy to be chased as Heather chased other boys.

It was due to Heather, though, that she first found herself in Damien's arms. They were playing tennis when Damien strolled round the back of the house and, catching sight of him, Heather returned the ball to Victoria with no thought but to shine and win praise. It was wild and would have gone out of the court, but Victoria never did anything by halves, and she flung herself outwards to reach it.

She came down heavily, and for a second lay there winded, her leg painfully beneath her. Damien was there at once, his gaze no longer mocking.

'Are you all right?'

She nodded shakily, grimacing in pain as he helped her to her feet.

'Where do you hurt?'

He seemed anxious, and this time she just found herself staring into his eyes, until he gave her a little shake.

'Victoria!'

'I—I fell on my leg. It's all right, though.'

To prove it she stepped away, and promptly gasped with pain, even more colour leaving her face as he swept her up into his arms. He never even answered Heather's queries, but walked off into the house carrying Victoria very gently.

Her grandfather stopped on his way across the hall, his expression a mixture of amusement and surprise, his reply predictable as Damien said that Victoria had fallen.

'It comes of unsuitable activities with unsuitable companions!' he said unsympathetically, and Victoria looked quickly around, thankful that Heather was only just approaching the house. Her grandfather didn't care at all if he insulted her friends. He simply walked off, leaving her to it, and Damien was laughing too.

'You can put me down!' she informed him, and her temper only seemed to amuse him more.

'If you're sure you feel able to stand,' he murmured mockingly.

'I never asked you to lift me up!' she snapped. 'I would have been perfectly fine if you'd left me.'

'I imagined you'd hurt your leg,' Damien murmured with the same mocking look, as if she'd done it all deliberately to get him to carry her.

'I *have* hurt my leg! My leg is hurting now!' she said very loudly, and his laughter bubbled over as he gently put her on her feet, his arms still around her.

'Nobody would give a damn if I killed myself,' she complained bitterly, filled with temper and confusion, and his free hand fastened in her hair, making her meet his laughing gaze.

'Quite true,' he agreed solemnly. 'That's why Andrew is now phoning his long-suffering doctor, that's why Molly is tearing downstairs, and that's why I'm here holding an ungrateful girl who really wants spanking!'

He sounded serious, but his eyes were laughing, and she blushed furiously.

'I—I'm sorry, Damien,' she confessed miserably, back to pleading with him as usual.

'Oh, I think I can survive an attack from you, princess,' he murmured softly and, to her amazement, he bent and kissed her, right at the corner of her mouth, and the only cool eyes there were Heather's, who had come in at just the wrong moment.

When Joel came she was glad to get out of the house. It was getting to be like a time-machine, and it only worked for the past. She could well do without the past. Joel drove her into town, tucking her hand under his arm as they walked about. It was like old times, and for one brief moment she was almost happy.

The town had come on enormously since she had been a child. It was rather grand in places, the old Victorian houses taken over and modernised carefully by people who worked miles away in the city. Even some of the stone terrace-houses had been given the same treatment, by people who preferred to live on the edge of the clean moorland than live close to work.

Tourists came too, because the moors were well-known, but even tourism would not save the ordinary people if anything happened to the textile mills. They relied, as they had always done, on Kendal and Hunt, the life-blood of the valley. Damien had made sure that they were safe. Everything was updated, competitive. Her grandfather had always had complete trust in Damien's business acumen, and he had watched with satisfaction the modernisation that had been slipped in so smoothly these last few years. He had told her about it in his letters, spoken of it at length when he had come down to see her.

Damien had other business interests. He was more wealthy than all of them, but his roots were here even so, his determination as strong as her grandfather's had been that the names of their families would never be torn from the sky and the mills demolished or sold.

Things would be very different now, though, because there was no longer a Kendal. She was the last of them and she intended to sell. Not even for her grandfather would she face life with Damien constantly in and out of her sight. What she would do about Molly she hadn't yet thought, but as for herself, she must get away soon.

Since yesterday she had never stopped thinking about him. She grimaced wryly. When had she *ever* stopped thinking about him? He was woven into the fabric of her existence, a thorn in the flesh—he always had been.

She shook herself angrily out of her mood and concentrated on Joel. If only Damien had been as kind, as gentle as his brother. If only she had felt nothing but quiet companionship with Damien. Everything she did was because of Damien. She had left this valley because of him—her only way of cheating him and her grandfather when she had discovered just what they had in mind. She was stunned that they had not known her better. Anxiety came back to her face as she remembered that the will reading was today. What had Damien wanted to talk about first, this morning? Well, she was out with Joel, and she wasn't about to sit meekly indoors waiting for Damien to call!

The feeling of being watched grew on her as she and Joel stopped for coffee, but she never turned. Lots of people would find her return fascinating. Maybe they, too, would think what Damien thought: that she had simply run out on her grandfather, and that now she was back to get all she could. The feeling was overpowering, though, and she gave in after a minute, turning her head carefully, not really surprised to see Damien.

He was in the doorway behind her, standing perfectly still, his hands in his pockets, his grey jacket pushed back as he watched her. His eyes held hers as she struggled for composure, a satisfaction on his face that she had felt the need to turn and look at him. Nobody else had ever been able to do that to her. He seemed to give out powerful waves that always reached her, and he had always known it. She would have to learn to do better than this. She simply turned away.

She hadn't even managed to get her breathing under control before he was towering over them both.

'Damien! Come and join us.' Joel sounded a little startled, but not as startled as he became.

'No, thanks, I'm here to relieve you of your burden.' His hand came to Victoria's arm and he pulled her to her feet, his eyes on her and not on his brother, even though Joel made protests. 'She had an appointment with me this morning and she knew it. One of these days you'll find out just exactly what your little playmate is like.'

'Let go of me!' Victoria ordered in a low voice, her face flushing as other customers heard the taunting voice and looked across with deep interest. 'I'm with Joel and I'm staying here.'

'If you require a scene, I guarantee one,' Damien informed her quietly. 'You're with me or you're with no one at all.'

'Now look here, Damien——'

Joel was on his feet too, but Damien was utterly unbending.

'Keep out of this, Joel,' he advised. 'Victoria and I have some unfinished business. You'll know all when the time comes.'

'I'll go, Joel,' Victoria said quietly. 'I don't fancy a scene.'

'Not unless you're making it yourself,' Damien remarked softly, turning to the door, and she noticed with mounting annoyance that the interested spectators hastily got on with their coffee. Damien Hunt was always daunting, and they hadn't worked out whether he was angry or amused. Neither had she, but there was a certain steel in his grip that promised trouble. She followed him out, and Joel came too, but he never had the chance to speak.

'See you later!' Damien just bundled Victoria into his car, and waved at Joel as he drove off.

'You high-handed, arrogant——'

'So you decided to do your own thing as usual?' he murmured, as if she weren't speaking at all. 'I imagined we had a meeting planned for this morning. I've been racing around looking for you, not considering for one moment that you'd be out taking coffee and enjoying yourself straight after Andrew's funeral.'

'What I do is none of your damned business!' she said shortly, finding the courage to look straight at him. 'As for enjoying myself, even searching my mind minutely, I can't come up with one time when I enjoyed myself in this place.'

His smile was twisted, sceptical.

'I remember when you certainly appeared to enjoy being with me, although you were always a little anxious, weren't you?'

'I have good instincts! What did you want to talk to me about, anyway?'

'I considered yesterday, judging by the look on your face, that you couldn't take another blow. Apparently, as usual, I was wrong. I constantly forget that you're hard, that the beautiful, delicate looks are deceptive. Let's leave it. Just remember the will is going to be read at eleven o'clock. It's almost that now. Were you about to duck out of it? Of course, I'll be quite willing to represent you, if you like,' he mocked. 'That way, there's no need for you to be there. I'll simply tell you later.'

'No way!' Victoria snapped. 'Your days of telling are over. Don't forget that I'm all Kendal. Now that grandfather is dead, I take his place!'

He stopped the car in the drive, his blue eyes seriously intent on her angry face.

'Don't say anything you'll regret later, Victoria,' he advised quietly. 'It's all too late now.'

'It was always too late!' She turned away abruptly, getting out to hide her face as tears threatened unexpectedly. 'There isn't a single plan you can make that will affect me at all—there never was.'

'The names still flare across the valley. My name is there beside yours. Everything I do will affect you.' He got out too, coming to tower over her and look down at her, but she kept her head turned away very carefully.

'Not for much longer. I already know what I'm going to do. You can buy me out, Damien. You can take down the name Kendal and have exactly what you've always wanted—everything! I'm leaving here. I've done well and I don't need this valley. Maybe I'll use some of my money to start an agency of my own.'

'You'll stay,' he informed her quietly. 'You'll find that you're staying right here with me.'

'We're back to that?' She tried to sound scornful, but her face was white and he noticed. 'You haven't got a co-conspirator now, Damien!'

'I never had. I usually make my own mind up about things. The conspiracy was in your own strange mind.'

'I've never had cause to doubt it—I wasn't a child,' Victoria bit out. 'I don't want you taking over my decisions again.'

'Who do you imagine is taking them over, then?' he asked quietly. 'Lloyd? That simpering little photographer friend, or one of your many lovers?'

'Rather anyone than you,' she said bitterly. 'But, for your information, I'll do exactly as I like. I'll do my own thinking!'

'Oh, you always have done as you like, but you never did think very straight,' he taunted. 'Left to you, we'd soon be in liquidation. You've only grown in size since you were a child. You've not grown in any other way.'

He reached forward and grasped her shoulders fiercely, his fingers biting into her flesh even through the jacket of her suit.

'Inside, you're still a spoiled child—just what Andrew made you!' he grated. He was suddenly angry, not mocking at all, but she fought back.

'A brat!' she reminded him. 'Don't forget that!'

'I see that you haven't,' he murmured, his eyes narrowing. 'It was a long time ago. Hurt, did it?' He looked down at her, tilting her face when she would have pulled away. 'Yes, you're still all of that,' he muttered impatiently. 'Silky hair like moonlight, weird, changing green eyes, a stubborn mouth and a bitter determination to have your own way at all costs.'

'If I'm bitter, then you made me so!'

She was starting to tremble madly, and he felt it, his gaze roaming over her face.

'How could I have made you bitter?' he asked slowly, drawing her closer. 'You're the most desirable brat I know, for so many reasons.' His smile was derisive, his eyes intently on her face until all her colour faded away.

'I can remember the reasons!' She glared at him, but he smiled scornfully.

'I remember too,' he informed her softly. 'I'm going to see to it that you don't forget. You're here to stay, Victoria. Get used to being with me. Get used to being in my arms. It's where you're going to end up, because it's absolutely necessary.'

He pulled her completely into his arms then, his lips finding hers ruthlessly, plundering her mouth, his hard arms making her struggles useless. There was disdain in his kiss, and she fought back wildly until he suddenly changed his tactics, his mouth beginning to coax her, his arms softening until her heart began to beat frantically against his own. He didn't care at all if Molly was watching from the house.

'Kiss me back, you fair-haired little witch!' he breathed against her lips, and for a moment she wanted to, her whole body trembling with desire.

Memory saved her, and she stiffened, her eyes darkening to an olive green with anger.

'Incredible,' he mocked. 'I didn't know there were so many shades of green. I'm going to have hours of pleasure watching those eyes change colour.'

'You're going to have nothing at all!' she assured him breathlessly, still trying to pull free.

'I'm going to have everything. Sorry, but there it is. You weren't much more than fifteen when your fate was decided. I'm about to collect.'

'Over my dead body!' she snapped, pulling free as he slackened his hold.

'That's not how I want it,' he murmured, his blue eyes skimming over her and resting on the rapid rise and fall of her breasts. 'I want it as it is right now, full of life and passion.'

'And hatred,' she said wildly.

'If necessary. It wouldn't bother me too much. Whatever you're like inside, you're really something again on the outside.'

'You don't have to pretend any more,' Victoria said coldly. 'You can have Kendal and Hunt. Simply buy me out.'

There was a frightening look of triumph about him, and he turned away suddenly, urging her to the steps. 'Almost eleven o'clock,' he reminded her softly. 'I'll see you after the reading.'

'The will is my grandfather's. It has nothing whatever to do with you.'

'You'll need me. Naturally, I'll be there. I always have been there when you needed me.'

She felt suddenly frightened. He knew something she didn't, and it could only be to her disadvantage. She stiffened and walked away towards the steps.

'I suppose Joel told you that he's going to Japan for me?' he suddenly shot out at her. 'I'm driving him down to the airport tomorrow afternoon. I think he wants you to join him for dinner tonight. I don't imagine he got the chance to ask, as you left so swiftly. He'll ring you, no doubt.'

'Why are you sending Joel away?' She swung to face him, a little shiver of fear creeping over her at the thought that Damien was isolating her from help.

He gave a peculiar smile.

'I'll be too busy to go for a while. I have things to do here.' His eyes skimmed over her as she turned and walked to the house. 'You walk beautifully,' he added softly. 'Like a dream. How much do you get paid down there?'

She told him quite flatly and he whistled in surprise.

'Hell! You don't come cheap, do you?'

'No, I don't. Not in any way at all.'

She stared at him coolly, and for a second his blue eyes looked shocked, colour flared over his cheekbones, then his mouth tightened with fury.

'You'll come any way I want you!' he bit out. 'I won't be paying for the privilege either!'

'Don't count me in your plans,' Victoria warned him. 'We live in modern times and I'm not bound to a name. Plenty of men have asked me to marry them.'

'Poor devils. They'll have to look elsewhere, won't they? Your future is pretty well established.'

She didn't answer, but turned and walked inside without a further word; of course, he followed. Short of pushing him out physically, there was nothing she could do, and anyone who tried to remonstrate physically with Damien Hunt had to be mad. She was not yet that.

CHAPTER THREE

Mr Gresham was already there, and Molly was hovering around anxiously, unsure for once how to cope. He had told her to be present, as she was mentioned in the will, but she had flatly refused.

'He's in the library,' she finished, her face set in determined lines, and Damien took over before Victoria could speak.

'Have coffee with me, Molly,' he suggested. 'You can be told all about things later—it's not necessary for you to be there. In any case, what Victoria is about to hear is very private.'

Victoria tried not to appear worried, but, whatever she was going to hear, she was quite sure it would not be good. Why was Damien so devilishly pleased with himself? There was no mistaking the look in his eyes.

She soon found out why. Mr Gresham seemed to dwell on things that were not at all important. She had been left the house and contents outright, to do with as she wished. There was a certain amount of money, not too much, but a few thousand. That surprised her a little. She knew her grandfather's ideas on money that sat about doing nothing. She hadn't expected to be in receipt of any liquid assets.

'You'll—er—you'll already know about the company, the shares and so forth?' Mr Gresham said hopefully, his eyes a little wary at the other side of thick spectacles.

'I don't know how many there are,' Victoria said sensibly. 'I have no idea of their present value either. I imagine you're going to enlighten me?'

He shuffled his papers, and then looked back at her in embarrassment.

'I had assumed that someone...your grandfather had...but, still, he never did hold with women in business, which, considering this modern day and age, just goes to show how wrong——'

'Mr Gresham, please!' Victoria said, becoming increasingly anxious. 'I know all about my grandfather's old-fashioned opinions. Let's get to the shares, please. I'm now half of Kendal and Hunt. Tell me about it.'

'The fact is, my dear Victoria...' he said quietly '...the fact is, you're not half of anything yet. Your grandfather should have told you all this. Apart from the bequests I've mentioned, you get nothing more until you're thirty, or until you—er—marry Mr Hunt, that is—er—Mr Damien Hunt. The moment that you do, or, failing that, the moment you reach the age of thirty, all your grandfather's shares, the Kendal shares, revert to you. The one proviso is that the name Kendal will always be there. Should you marry Mr Hunt, the names are to be hyphenated discreetly—er—Kendal-Hunt, you see? If you marry anyone else you must keep your own name.'

'I see. And until then?'

How she was managing to speak at all, Victoria did not know. Damien had known, just as he had always known. Nothing had changed, after all. This was what he had wanted to tell her. This was what he had decided to let her find out the hard way.

'Until then? Well, naturally, Mr Hunt, being the senior partner now, takes control of everything. Dividends will, of course, be paid to you and, as I say, you have this house and the furniture plus a goodly sum. The rest waits, and naturally you have no say over anything at all until you——'

He stopped in embarrassment, and then murmured on quietly, giving her advice about the money—the loose

change, as it were. A few thousand and the house! Her
grandfather had said nothing of this, but she knew it
had always been in his mind. He hadn't mellowed away
from it.

Victoria stood up slowly and carefully, walking out of
the room and making for her own bedroom, leaving Mr
Gresham to find his own way out, or maybe Damien
would see him out? He controlled everything now, so
he might as well take over the family solicitor.

'Victoria!'

Damien's voice hit her like a volume of cold water,
but she kept going and never looked round. She heard
him walk into the study—her grandfather's study—and
then she shut her bedroom door and sat down, shocked
and trembling.

Not that she should have been bewildered. Damien
and her grandfather never lost a battle. She thought she
had escaped, put Damien firmly in his place, but they
had merely changed their tactics and her grandfather had
said nothing at all in over six years!

What did it matter, after all? She had already decided
what she was going to do. With the sale of this house
and the furniture, much of it antiques, she would be
perfectly comfortable. She would buy a place in London
and go back to her old escape—modelling. It had worked
before. The thought of the future frightened her, though,
and what frightened her most was the idea of Damien's
right to have anything at all to do with her life. She might
be able to go back to London and stay there, but for all
the time until she inherited, the thought of Damien would
hang like a sword over her head. Six more years of dread
and bitterness. She wasn't sure if she could face it.

She stared out of the window, but saw nothing. There
was an odd feeling of unreality—as if she had been flung
headlong into the past. It had all been around this time

of the year before, only then it had been her birthday—
her eighteenth, with magic in the air...

For the first time it was a very grown-up party—even
her grandfather had acknowledged the need for that.
Everybody had come but, most of all, *Damien* had come.
She hadn't expected him, because he was already
chairman of so many companies that he was hardly ever
at home, but somehow there had been a great difference
in her feelings for him since that time, a year before,
when he had lifted her up and carried her to the house.

His attitude to her, too, was changed. She no longer
felt the need to defend herself. She felt quite beautiful
sometimes, when those blue eyes smiled and lanced over
her. It was like discovering a wonder that had been there
unnoticed all her life. Every day was breathtaking with
the thought that he might suddenly appear, and she knew
without being told that she had changed into another
person.

In spite of her determination to be very sensible, she
had been watching for him all evening, her heart taking
on an extraordinary pounding when he came. He arrived late, and was almost immediately closeted with her
grandfather, but just the thought that he was in the house
was enough to bring colour to her face and a sparkle to
her eyes—although he hadn't even looked at her as he
came in.

He came out of the study unexpectedly when she was
standing talking to Jeremy Lloyd, and he swung her into
his arms and the rhythm of the dance before she had
time to get breathless with anxiety, and she knew that
she *did* get breathless with anxiety because, in spite of
her newly discovered fascination with him, he was still
Damien: untouchable, imperious and way above her in
everything.

'I didn't know you'd arrived,' she lied quickly, striving to be as sophisticated as she could, quite sure that Damien was only accustomed to glossy women.

'Didn't you?' His slightly mocking smile made her turn her face away in embarrassment.

'There are a lot of people here,' she said unsteadily. 'I can't keep an eye on everybody.'

'Just keep an eye on me,' he taunted. Colour flooded into her face, and he relented, his cool teasing stopping at once. 'Eighteen,' he said softly, looking down at her with a smile. 'I suppose everyone has already told you how beautiful you look in that dress?'

'Yes.' She felt downcast at his tone. It seemed to be slightly patronising, as if he didn't recognise that to-night she was eighteen and grown-up. The jade green of the dress coloured her eyes as she glanced up at him defiantly, her eyes sparkling green. 'I don't mind hearing it again, though.'

He laughed softly and tightened his arm around her waist, his other hand holding hers against his chest.

'You're beautiful—more beautiful every time I see you. What more can I say?' She was vaguely disappointed. Somehow she had expected a deep reaction from him, maybe anger at her sharp tone, or even perhaps a flirting reply. She had got neither.

'Are you sulking?' He lowered his head and whispered in her ear, sending delicious shivers down her spine. She could only shake her head, and his hand tightened on hers. 'Do I get a birthday kiss, then?'

She looked up at him quickly, but his eyes were dancing with amusement and she knew he didn't mean it. He had never kissed her, apart from that small kiss last year. He was mocking again, and she looked at him reproachfully.

'I don't kiss all and sundry!' she managed tartly, but he still smiled into her eyes.

'I'm glad to hear it, because I'm going to London and off to Japan on the first flight out. I won't be able to keep an eye on you.'

There was still the teasing tone, but his gaze was intent on her face, and he couldn't mistake her expression.

'But you only just got back from America!' Her eyes were wide and disappointed, sophistication and defiance completely forgotten. 'I—we hardly ever see you.'

'I can remember when you would have been happy to run quite a few miles to avoid me,' he reminded her, noticing her little slip. His looks suddenly softened as he glanced over her flushed face. 'Anyway, I can't build an empire by sitting here looking at you.'

'Why do you want to build an empire?' There was suddenly excitement in the evening again, at the idea that he would think of just sitting and looking at her. 'You've got half of Kendal and Hunt. We're all rich.'

He didn't answer; instead he swung her to the door.

'I'll have to go. Come and see me off,' he ordered. 'I've already said my goodbyes to your grandfather.'

She didn't want to see him off, she wanted him to stay, but she followed him outside, breathless when he insisted that she go right to his car.

'Your present. I almost drove off with it,' he said quietly, handing her a small box. 'Open it when I've gone.'

Victoria was miserable almost to the point of tears. This was the only reason he had wanted her to come down to the car. The magic suddenly went out of everything.

'All right.' She looked up at him with a tentative smile, quite prepared to beg a little. 'I'll do without a present if you'll stay for the rest of the evening and go on the next plane.'

It was daring, taking into account that this was Damien she was speaking to, and it didn't do any good either.

'No chance!' He looked down at her and laughed before reaching out, taking her by the waist and drawing her towards him.

'Come with me,' he suggested softly.

It took her breath away and the blue eyes locked with hers.

'You—you don't mean it,' she whispered shakily. 'Don't tease me all the time, Damien.'

His eyes narrowed at her distressed look, and he pulled her close to him, looking down into her upturned face.

'I mean it,' he said quietly. His eyes roamed over her face. 'It's quite mad, but I mean it, though if you agreed I would probably say no. Kiss me goodbye!' he ordered, tilting her chin.

She stood on tiptoe. She was trembling, but she obediently kissed his cheek, her heart fluttering madly now that the forlorn hope had come to pass, but she never managed to escape.

'I don't think that's going to do at all,' he murmured. 'I really think I need more than that.'

He caught her close, his hand holding her face as his lips closed over hers. Surprise was laced with fear and she gasped, her parted lips an invitation he did not refuse. His mouth opened over hers, and she was immediately swept into a drowsy, sexual demand as he kissed her slowly and repeatedly, draining her sweetness for long minutes.

It was overwhelming. The excitement led her almost to the point of fainting, and she was trembling violently when he lifted his head and steadied her, his blue eyes burning through her.

'Don't forget me,' he murmured against her hair, as her head fell forward. 'I'll be back.'

She looked up and he held her fast, his eyes on her dazed face.

'I honestly think you'd better go back inside—otherwise, I'll take you with me anyway,' he warned quietly.

There was a peculiar husky sound to his voice and a feeling of tension in his arms that made her realise he meant it. She could still feel her lips burning. Her skin felt as if it were on fire, and she only moved because he made her move, turning her back to the house.

It was only when she arrived safely in her room that she realised she was still clutching the box. She opened it, her heart beating wildly as she saw the gift. It was an emerald on a golden chain, the most beautiful thing she had ever possessed in her life, and she clutched it to her, her face radiant with happiness. She spent the rest of the evening on a dazed cloud, happy and scared all at the same time. The next day a van delivered flowers in a long, elegant box. Inside were two dozen roses—red ones—and a card with just one thing written on it: 'Damien'.

More than the kisses, more than the expensive emerald, the flowers touched her romantic young heart. He had thought of her before he went. He had stopped to order flowers. He wanted her. All the things that Heather had told her about men came flooding into her mind, but they did not disgust her. How could they? This was Damien, and he was different from other men.

She spent the week walking on an airy cloud as golden as the chain hidden around her neck, nobody knowing about it but Damien and herself, and she took a chance she would never normally have dared to take. When Joel phoned from university, to have a word and wish her a belated happy birthday, he told her that Damien was coming home on Friday, and she decided to go down to meet him herself.

It took a lot of courage. She had to tell her grandfather in the first place, and in the second place she was still worried about Damien. He had never thought twice about it when he wanted to reprimand her, and he may feel that it was very forward of her. Maybe he had suddenly felt a little mad?

She passed the first hurdle with astonishing ease. Her grandfather merely looked closely at her and asked if she needed any money, his only rule being that she go the whole way by train. Molly was more shocked. Molly was obsessed by the distance, not being any sort of traveller herself, and she was more than a little disturbed at Victoria's carefully blithe attitude about this trip to meet Damien off the plane.

It didn't matter. She felt she had to make some sort of gesture to show that she wasn't scared. He had really wanted to take her with him. If he asked her again, she would go. She wasn't a child. She knew what Damien had been feeling when he kissed her like that.

She got the probable time of his arrival and planned around that, but she was right back to being scared as she saw him come through Customs. She had positioned herself where he would see her, or at least where she would see him, and, when she did see him, her heart almost stopped with fright, every romantic thought leaving her.

He looked tired and grim, the lips that had kissed her so drowsily now in one straight line. He had his bag in his hand, another slung over his shoulder. He looked like an irritated, wealthy businessman and nothing to do with her at all. He was the Damien she had respected and feared all her life.

Victoria wanted to fade into the background, to travel home and pretend it had all been a joke, that she had been to see friends, but she didn't get the chance. She had positioned herself to be seen and he saw her.

He stopped dead in his tracks, his blue eyes coming to life, flaring over her face, her fair hair, her slender figure in the flowing green dress she wore. She had worn that colour deliberately, and she wondered uneasily if he knew. She felt as if she were behaving badly, and he was sure to tell her so.

His eyes narrowed as he walked over to her, standing to look down at her anxious face.

'You're here for me? You're not by any chance waiting for the arrival of some foreign dignitary?'

'Maybe I shouldn't have come——' she began hesitantly, avoiding his eyes, but he tilted her chin and forced her to look at him, his eyes piercingly blue.

'What did Andrew say about this adventure?' he asked softly, seemingly fascinated by her blushes.

'He—Grandfather just insisted that I came by train.'

'And what else?' he asked sharply.

'Nothing.' She couldn't understand why he should be so annoyed with her grandfather too, unless he thought she should have been supervised more. It made her feel childish.

'Let's go, then.' He bent and kissed her cheek. 'You've welcomed me, now let's get out of here.'

His car was parked at the airport, and she was still trembling as he opened the door and motioned her inside. His eyes were coldly blue and she knew he was angry— he just wasn't telling her off right at once. He was probably angry with her grandfather too for letting her come. He still thought she was a child, apparently—a very forward child, who had had the temerity to act like this.

The traffic was terrible, and that did nothing to relax him, either. In fact, he never spoke at all until they were out of London and heading north.

'Are you hungry?' He was staring straight ahead, his face cold and distant.

'A little.' She searched around for some sort of conversation. 'What do you normally do? About eating after a trip, I mean.'

'Normally,' he said tightly, 'I stay in my London flat overnight and get some rest, recover my temper and so forth. Normally, though, I'm not met by an anxious green-eyed teenager. If I *am* met, it's by someone who is prepared to go to the flat with me and cook me a meal. I've never been met before by a young girl who merely does as she likes.'

'You—you asked me to go with you before you——'

'A fit of madness from which I've totally recovered.'

'I can cook you a meal, if—if you're hungry,' Victoria stated with more firmness than she felt, trying to ignore everything else, her heart sinking when she realised he was met by some woman more often than not. The flowers took on a different meaning and she was ashamed of the way she had rushed to meet him. He had probably just been amused and sent the flowers as a joke. 'I—can cook you meal just like anyone who meets you normally.'

'The lady then expects to stay at the flat,' he murmured mockingly.

'I can get a train home after I've cooked for you. I'm quite able to look after myself.'

'Are you? You're quite able to place yourself in a dangerous situation!' he snapped.

'Well, I didn't, did I?' she flared, turning away and looking out the window, too miserable now to want to speak.

'You think you're safe with me?'

'I expect so. I'm quite used to being a nuisance to you and being reprimanded. So what's new?'

He began to laugh softly, some of the tension leaving his shoulders, and in the gathering dusk he pulled into the deserted car park of a hotel.

'We'll eat here,' he informed her, adding as her eyes widened in renewed anxiety, 'then we'll go straight home.

I'll not teach you a lesson this time. Anyway, I'm too damned tired!'

All through the meal she was silent with embarrassment, her lighter-than-air feeling gone completely. He had called her an anxious teenager, and she could tell from his mocking smile that he meant it. He also still thought that she did anything she chose to do, regardless of her grandfather's orders. She was the only one with romantic thoughts. The kisses at her birthday worried her, but she didn't understand men, after all. Damien spoke quietly, but not very often, and she was too tight inside to do more than mutter her answers. There was something a little threatening about him, and a few of Heather's remarks swam like sharks to the top of her mind.

It was quite dark when they went back to the car, and she struggled nervously with her seat belt until he sighed in exasperation.

'I'll do that!' he said, quite sharply, and tears spilled over on to her cheeks, a mixture of humiliation and bewilderment. He wasn't even glad to see her.

'Don't cry, Victoria.'

Even in the darkness he knew she was crying silently, and he made no move to fasten her safely in. His voice was quiet, and his hand stroked her wet face, his touch gentle in spite of his taut voice.

'I'm tired, angry and frustrated,' he said softly. 'I'm not good company.'

'It—it's my fault,' she assured him shakily. 'I don't know why I did it. Naturally you're angry with me for making you alter your plans. If you had a woman waiting——'

'I'm not angry with you!' he rasped, jerking away stiffly, sitting back and staring out at the hotel lights that now seemed to penetrate the car. 'There was no woman waiting and I'm angry with myself, not you.'

'I don't understand.' She dried her eyes and looked at him mournfully. His handsome face was tight, the blue eyes that had begun to smile at her over the last year were now back to being distant and chilly.

'That's why I'm frustrated!' he bit out, turning on her suddenly when she shrank away at the harsh sound of his voice. 'Don't *do* that!' he snapped, and then his face softened miraculously. 'Oh, Victoria,' he murmured, 'come here to me.' He reached for her and pulled her across into his arms, looking down at her for a moment. 'If you knew how I felt when I saw you at the airport, you'd have good reason to be scared,' he said quietly.

'I knew you were surprised and annoyed,' she whispered, looking up at him.

'Surprised, yes,' he confessed softly. 'I was all of that. Not annoyed, though. This is what I was thinking about—how I felt.'

He lifted her towards him, kissing her face, her eyes and the smooth line of her chin, before his lips closed over her own hungrily.

It was just like before, the feeling she had begun to imagine she had dreamed. His kisses were sensuous and slow, demanding, and she went spinning out of all reality as his arm cradled her head and his free hand stroked her neck, then moved down gently to her breast.

'Damien!'

There was so much pleasure that her heart seemed to be bursting, but he went right on holding her and touching her, his hand light and teasing, until her arms wound around his neck and she began to kiss him back.

'My little Victoria! You grew up!'

He crushed her against him, kissing every part of her he could reach: her face, her eyes, her lips, the smooth skin of her neck, and the soft contours of her breasts through the silken material of her dress. His hands caressed her hungrily, and when he lifted his head his eyes seemed to burn her, as her breath struggled to be more than a sobbing sound deep in her throat.

'Do you understand now? Do you understand that you're mine?' he asked thickly. 'I want you, Victoria. You were made for me, and I'll not let anyone else have you, whoever it is, I need you too much myself.'

She looked up at him with dazed eyes. Nobody had ever held her and kissed her like that. Nobody had touched her, and even now his hand was heavily possessive on her breast. It was all magical and new.

'I'm frightening you?' he asked softly. He suddenly smiled, his hand stroking her face, the tension draining out of him. 'Do you know I've been waiting for you for a very long time?'

She shook her head, her feelings no way under her own control, and he took her fingers and raised them to his lips.

'Marry me,' he said softly. 'Marry me soon. I don't want to go on waiting for you. I need you now, not later.'

'I—I don't know what to say,' she whispered. She had felt very young, and he had called her a teenager when he was angry—but now he had made her feel like a woman.

His lips moved over the softness of her palm, closing her fingers gently around the kiss.

'Think about it, and then say yes,' he suggested huskily. 'Say yes very soon. I want you with me, where I can see you all the time. Isn't that what you want, too?'

He looked deeply into her eyes, and she felt a great surge of happiness and excitement.

'Oh, Damien, yes! It *is* what I want too!'

He smiled slowly, his eyes roaming over her flushed face, before his lips stroked over hers. 'I won't have to kidnap you, then,' he teased gently, as he sat her up and fastened her into her seat.

'Would you have done?' she asked tremulously, still
shaken and trembling.

'Anything it takes, my beautiful little witch. It
wouldn't be the first time I've thought about it.'

'Oh!' Victoria gasped.

He suddenly laughed, and dropped a kiss on her
startled lips. 'Let's go before the idea takes hold of me
too much. You did offer to cook me a meal at my flat,
if you remember.'

'I—I'll go back with you. if you want me to,' she offered shakily, looking up at him.

For a moment his eyes narrowed, and then his
expression softened as his lips quirked with amusement.

'No. I prefer to have you legally. When I marry you,
there'll be no running away. Whatever happens, remember that,' he added softly, his face suddenly serious.

'I won't run away,' she whispered. 'I love you,' she
added, suddenly gloriously sure.

He looked at her for a long time, and then kissed her
deeply before starting the car, but he didn't say anything. He didn't say 'I love you, too', but she knew he
did. Damien would never kiss anyone like that unless he
loved them. She was almost beside herself with happiness. She would leave it to Damien to tell her grandfather, but she knew there would be no trouble. Damien
wouldn't allow it and he wanted her soon.

There was a vague fear to the magic a week later. It
was true that Damien spent all his time with her, took
her out to dinner, kissed her and behaved tenderly, but
there was an uneasiness about him that transmitted itself
to her, and her eyes were constantly on him, their gaze
worried. She didn't know if he had told her grandfather,
because nobody had mentioned it to her and she was
too young and shy to ask. It was all so new to her, and
Damien was older. She had no idea whether this was
normal or not, and she had nobody to confide in.

Finally it was all explained by her grandfather, without any questioning at all. He could not have failed to notice the time she had begun to spend with Damien, and it clearly pleased him, although he did not know the depth of her commitment.

'Well, I can see that all the planning paid off,' he said with satisfaction one morning after breakfast. 'I expect you'll be married soon, now. I never did hold with business being handed on to women, and now I can safely leave it all to Damien.'

'Are you talking about Kendal and Hunt, Grandfather?'

She had never thought about any inheritance. To her, at eighteen, her grandfather was almost immortal, but she had always known that she should be allowed to take some interest in the mills—that one day she would share responsibility with Damien and Joel.

'I am, Victoria,' he said firmly. 'There'll be no need for you to worry. I can hand everything over to Damien. Yes,' he sighed with satisfaction, 'it's all been very successful, all the planning worthwhile.'

She suddenly felt cold, a growing feeling of shock and disbelief.

'What planning?' She was almost whispering, but he didn't seem to notice.

'I've been preparing you for Damien for years!' he assured her, with the confidence that came from an age when women were merely chattels. He might have been her great-great-grandfather speaking. 'When your father died, Victoria, I knew that the line was finished. I want those names over the valley, though, and Damien has always agreed to that. He's ready to marry you now, I hear, and you're old enough at last.'

'He's—he's marrying me for—for the mills?' she asked, her icily cold hands clasped together, his sudden passion for her explained so cruelly. 'You've arranged my life between you?'

'He wants to marry you!' he said with a growl of anger at her question. 'He'd be mad not to. He has to marry one day, and he'll get everything when he marries you, providing he keeps the names there. In any case,' he added impatiently, 'he's wanted you for years—I'm not blind, girl!'

No, not blind, but wicked, unfeeling, cruel! Both of them were that, with their plans, their plotting—her life the pawn to be moved around, bargained for. Now she understood the kisses and the impatient haste. She understood why he had never talked of love, just wanting her. He had wanted her, all right! Damien was committed to this, an equal conspirator, and he was wanting to get it over with quickly so that he could get on with his life, wanting to marry her before she discovered what it was all about!

She left the house quietly early the next day, taking her things and leaving a note for her grandfather. She was going to friends in London, and she was not coming back. She simply disappeared. She was too humiliated to face Damien and accuse him. He was out of the country again, and she knew that when he came back he would want to talk about the wedding arrangements. There was no way that she would become part of a business deal.

She was tall, slender and beautiful, with a natural grace about her, and before the month was out she had already started on a new career in modelling. She had enough money of her own to take a flat and get all the photographs she needed, and already her childhood seemed to be light-years away, her beautiful face cool and controlled, the valley left behind for good.

Of course Damien found her. He went to her old school and got the names and addresses of every girl she had been friendly with, but she met him coldly. There was nothing of the trembling teenager about her at all. The shock of his duplicity and her few weeks facing the world on her own had given her a sheen of ice, and their parting was bitter and angry. She had almost thrown the golden chain with the emerald at his feet.

'I've no intention of marrying you and living in that dreary place. I don't need this bond of slavery, either,' she said coldly. 'I'm used to the bright lights. I intend to live here. I've come to my senses!'

He seemed to have no idea that her grandfather had told her anything, and the fact that she had agreed to marry him and then changed her mind made him rage wildly. She seemed to have confirmed his long-held opinion of her, and her humiliation and hurt were too great for her to confront him with her knowledge.

'One day,' Damien threatened, the golden chain in his hand, 'I'll hold you in my arms and you'll beg for this "bond of slavery". One day you'll ask me to forgive you.'

'Don't live in hope! Except for one brief spell of madness, I've always hated you. First impressions are supposed to be right.'

'So they are, you cold-hearted little brat! You're all your grandfather has.'

'No, I'm not! He has what he's always had—the mills, Kendal and Hunt. Nobody ever needed me, a mere girl.'

'Victoria,' he began more softly, but she was not about to be coaxed any more. She opened the door pointedly.

'Don't bother, Damien!' she snapped. 'I don't fall in the same hole twice.'

Her grandfather wrote to her, and then he came, but he did not beg for her return. She had his own stubborn nature and, in any case, he never denied that he and Damien, with their plotting, had planned her future without any thought of her happiness.

He had never explained her sudden departure to Damien, either, a course of inaction that was typical of him, and she made him promise that he would never tell Damien anything about her—not even that they wrote to each other and that he visited her. It appealed to his odd sense of humour. In any case, he had no idea that she loved Damien.

Damien had never come again to find her, and she knew as soon as she saw his face again that he would never forgive, and never cease to fight her. He wanted everything. Now he had everything, unless she either married him or waited patiently for her thirtieth birthday.

CHAPTER FOUR

VICTORIA didn't answer when he knocked on the door—she was still in the past, too stunned to make a move from the window, her eyes fixed on the names high above the valley.

'Victoria?'

Damien came in, stopping just inside the doorway when she never even turned.

'Victoria!' There was a suppressed violence in his voice that gained her attention, and she turned her head to look at him. He was taut, angry, the blue eyes blazing.

'What do you want?' she asked in an almost dreamy voice, her mind still suspended between memories of hurt and of passion.

'What I've always wanted!' he grated. 'I tried to tell you about the will—maybe I should have taken you aside and told you yesterday, but I thought you needed a rest, a chance to come to terms with Andrew's death. You didn't, obviously. You went right on doing what you want to do, even skipping out of this morning's meeting. Maybe now you'll see reason!'

'Reason?' she asked in angry surprise. 'I'm the last Kendal! If my father had lived, you would be dealing with him, not me. You want to see those names there forever, just as my grandfather did, but you want total control of everything. Well, you've got control. It's all yours, Damien. For now. When I finally inherit, I'll sell my half and, after this, I'll sell to an outsider!'

He strode forward angrily, grasping her arms and shaking her hard.

'Not while you and I are alive!' he rasped. 'The names are there and they'll stay. The only difference is that they'll move closer together. Kendal-Hunt is what Andrew wanted, and that's what he'll get.'

'Then do it!' she snapped, jerking free of him. 'Do it, hollow though it will be. You can have the satisfaction of it for a while.'

'Do you imagine I cheated Andrew?' he asked bitterly. 'How do you think I managed it?'

'I don't think you cheated, Damien,' she said wearily, turning away. 'Grandfather couldn't be either cheated or bullied. I recognise his fine machiavellian hand in the will. He told me clearly so many times that business was not for women. He obviously didn't intend to leave me with any choice.'

'Maybe he was waiting for everything to come right,' Damien said tightly. 'Maybe he was waiting for you to grow up. Is that why you ran away to London? Because he told you that? You were setting up on your own? Hell! I wanted to marry you, Victoria, so very much!'

'Stop trying to talk me round to anything!' she cried desperately, hating the way he could sound so hurt when it was all play-acting. 'I know why I was suddenly, after years of dislike, a desirable object in your eyes. I was suitable, a Kendal, the only one left—a girl who just might have a mind of her own and a desire to marry and get a name that was neither Kendal nor Hunt. Better still, I was eighteen and an idiot!'

'You're not eighteen now,' he said with a return to coldness. 'A marriage between us is what Andrew wanted, and it's what I want too. It should have happened long ago, but you can be quite sure it's going to happen now. London is a thing of the past, Victoria.' He suddenly looked less tense, his tone changing. 'You were always the most beautiful thing I had ever seen in my life; you still are. Marrying you is not going to be any hardship. I once told you that I wanted you. I still do. I'll settle for that.'

Victoria flushed, a feeling racing over her skin that she had never felt since Damien had held her so long ago. No other man had made her feel like Damien had. Even after all those years, she remembered it. She remembered why it had happened too.

'Oh, *please*, Damien!' she implored sarcastically. 'I remember. I also remember telling you that I don't step into the same hole twice.'

'And I remember telling you that one day you'd lie in my arms begging me to put that "bond of slavery" back around your neck,' he jeered softly. 'You will. I've got the mills and the names permanently, because I'm going to have you.'

'I'd love to know how you propose to go about it,' Victoria said drily, her temper and hurt under tight control now, her face calm, back to the way she had trained it long ago. Anger and hurt were bubbling just below the surface, though. She was no longer scared of Damien, but he was much too close to be ignored when all the past was washing around her. 'Obviously you knew all about this will, having helped to draft it. I can wait for my money, though.'

'And when it all boils down to it,' he said scathingly, 'that's all you care about, isn't it? Spoiled and pampered, cellophane-wrapped. You thought nothing of deserting Andrew, and now you want his money. There *is* no money, my spoiled beauty—not until you're thirty. That's a very long time, Victoria.'

'It doesn't matter one bit. I've lived perfectly well so far. I'll survive.'

'Do you imagine I'm going to take care of the Kendal holdings to see you marry some layabout and pass them on to his children? The mills go to my children—mine and yours when you marry me.'

'As if I would.' Victoria turned away, seeing the names now through a blur of unexpected tears. She had dreamed once of having Damien's children, children with jet black hair and brilliant blue eyes.

'I already know what I'm going to do,' she said steadily, pushing the memories back. 'I shall sell the house and furniture and go back to London. I like the bright lights, the nightlife——'

'And men leering at you,' he sneered insultingly. 'I'll stop you. Heaven knows, I owe that much to Andrew.'

'You'd have to lock me up,' she said with cold triumph, hearing the determination in his voice.

'Maybe I will,' he threatened quietly. 'I remember once that I thought of kidnapping you. At least that way you'd remain unmarried, though I suspect you're not what might be called virginal!'

He turned and walked out, and minutes later his sleek, red Ferrari turned down the drive and away to town. Pity the person who tried to stop him now. Victoria breathed a deep sigh and went to find Molly.

When she went to have dinner with Joel she told him all about it, and he was more puzzled than shocked.

'There's some mistake here, Vic,' he said slowly and thoughtfully. 'Damien may be many things, but he wouldn't agree to a will like that. You have every right to your inheritance now.'

Of course, Joel knew nothing of her youthful infatuation with Damien. He had been at university then. He had no idea that Damien had held her in his arms and kissed her breathless. Joel knew nothing of Damien's determination to marry her, either then or now. He knew that the mills were in Damien's hands for now, but he could not believe that Damien had known about the will. Victoria had no such doubt. Damien had told her he knew.

'I don't want you to speak to Damien about this, Joel,' she said firmly.

'I can't at the moment, because he's at a party with Heather Lloyd,' Joel muttered angrily, 'but I'm going to have trouble keeping my mouth shut when he drives me to London tomorrow.'

At a party with Heather Lloyd. Heather had always wanted to capture Damien, and now she was his secretary, close to him daily, and Joel thought there was something between them. She didn't doubt it. Heather had no qualms when she went after a man. Of course, he couldn't be captured permanently, not if he wanted everything to go on as before, the names drawn together for ever. She couldn't get rid of the thought of him with Heather, though, and she went home with a tight pain inside that seemed to grow the more she tried to shrug it off. She couldn't get Damien's face out of her mind, either. It had never been out of her mind since she was a child.

She had talked things over with Molly, and they had both decided that they had no desire to stay on at the big, old house. For the time being, Molly would move in with her sister, and Victoria would move into a hotel. It was only for a few days, because she would have to get back to her job.

It wasn't what either of them really wanted, but Victoria knew she had to get away from Damien and back to London. Molly would never go with her, she knew that, but even though she was now a top model, her face on the cover of many magazines, if she delayed too long there would be no job left for her. Others were always pressing behind. It was tiring and competitive, and not too safe.

She moved the next day, taking the few things she needed and staying overnight at the best hotel the town offered. On Sunday she would go up to the house and sort out her clothes and the rest of the things she intended to keep. After that, the agents could take over. It was a terrible wrench to think of parting with the house that had been in her family for so long, but there was little alternative. She could get away now, or stay and become a stubborn, bitter old maid, seeing Damien finally marry someone else.

It was raining on Sunday, the sky overcast, a chill wind blowing off the moors and, having arrived, she didn't really want to turn the key and go inside. It was a place filled with memories, not all of them happy, and it took a deal of courage to go into the dark hall and walk around the lonely rooms.

She finally made her way upstairs and busied herself in sorting out her clothes, ready to make the first of several trips to her flat. There were things here she hadn't worn for years, because they hadn't been suitable for her life-style, and she looked at them critically now, trying to summon up the courage to throw them away, and not let them bring back memories of where she had been when she wore them. Damien was always in the picture in such thoughts.

How long could she stay in the hard world she had built for herself? Could she continue to don the mask of indifference again, and view the world from cold, glittering eyes? The thought that she might not be able to keep going frightened her. She had always been shy, always felt just slightly superfluous to requirements, a legacy from her grandfather's heavy ways. London was the only place where she could lose herself, and she was trained for nothing else but what she did now.

From a common-sense point of view she should stay here and learn the business, then take over her share when the time came, but the thought was no sooner in her mind than she thrust it out. Damien was here. She had to get away, as far and as quickly as possible. She

knew him well for what he was, and there was no way
he could be allowed to get close to her, to bring on the
old heartache. She knew perfectly well that she still felt
a quick leap of her heart when she saw him.

A noise disturbed her and she stood still, listening.
Someone was in the house. She tried to remember if she
had relocked the door, and she was fairly certain that
she had not. It was not her habit to lock the door when
she came in—Molly had always done that at night. She
looked round quickly for some route of escape, because
she knew exactly where everyone was today: Molly was
visiting other relatives, Joel was in Japan, Damien had
been invited to the Lloyds' house—Heather had rung to
tell her this news with a sound of triumph in her voice
that told how the party had gone. Of course, Jeremy
Lloyd would never just walk in here, he was much too
polite.

Victoria backed away from the door, her eyes wide.
She told herself that this was ridiculous, but the valley
was not as it had been, and crime was growing everywhere. She felt utterly trapped, mentally berating herself
for leaving the door unlocked, her eyes searching the
room for some kind of weapon.

'Victoria?'

Damien simply walked into the room, and she suddenly realised that she was trembling violently, almost
ready to scream. This old house, her grandfather's death,
the recent upsets, had left her very vulnerable and
nervous.

She was utterly incapable of answering immediately,
and he stood in the doorway looking at her.

'What are you doing here alone with the front door
unlocked?' he demanded, as if he had every right to take
her task.

Fury rose over fear for a second, and she flew at him,
wanting to attack him physically for the hurt he had

brought in the past and the arrogance of his attitude now. She was across the room before he realised her intention, her hands raised to attack him.

'How dare you walk in here as if you own the place?' she stormed, launching herself at him. 'This is my house! You have no right——'

He looked utterly surprised, but he caught her almost in mid-flight, trapping her arms and stopping her impetus by crushing her against his powerful frame.

'What's the matter with you, you little vixen?' he snapped. 'You've not changed much, have you? Still demanding explanations, still pursuing your own course! I've been coming here all my life. I saw your car and called out. You never answered. How was I to know you were all right?'

'I'm always all right!' she raged, struggling furiously. 'I've always been able to take care of myself. You're supposed to be at the Lloyds'!'

'Ah!' He eased his hold on her a little, his eyes losing their puzzled and angry look. 'You were scared.'

'I was not!' she lied vehemently. 'You have no right to be in this house now, so you can just get out of it.'

'I frightened you,' he said quietly, speaking as if she had never answered him. 'You had worked out exactly where everyone was and you were afraid. What the devil made you imagine I was at the Lloyds' house?' he suddenly added curtly, letting her go and standing back.

'Heather said——'

'So you're back in touch with your old friend?' he enquired scathingly. 'Was it worth the phone call? What other information did you wheedle out of her?'

'She called me, not the other way around. As to wheedling information out of her, there's not a thing about this place that I would want to know. You're welcome to each other—like finds like, finally!' Victoria snapped out.

'So, you've been hearing the gossip? Heather knows exactly where she stands with me,' he murmured ironically. 'She knows I intend to marry you.'

'No, thank you!' Victoria tensed and turned away. 'I just came to get the things I want from here. I have a flat in London, and obviously I'll not be able to take many things. The agent can deal with the rest. What you do doesn't even begin to concern me.'

'There's room for anything you want to keep if you move across the valley to my house,' he reminded her mockingly. 'You're going to end up there eventually, so why bother to clear things away?'

'I don't find this at all amusing, Damien.' Victoria turned on him, her temper seething, a good shield from the suddenly violent pain she felt at the thought of Heather with him. 'There's nothing to keep me here now, and when Molly is settled I'll be off back to London, so let's not get into any discussion.'

'I've told you what I intend.'

He stood looking at her implacably, and she was suddenly filled with a great desire to upset that cool control.

'If I stay it will be to get to know the business—and take a hand in it. You may find me more of a nuisance now than you ever did when I was a teenager.'

'You think so?' The blue eyes mocked her. 'You're good for one thing only, and that's what I'm going to have. As to the business, you have no rights at all—except to collect your dividends and wait. Andrew tied it all up. He knew you well enough. We produce top-class textiles, of world renown. With you sticking your nose into things, we'd be turning out cheap and tawdry purple satin for lurid undies.'

'I'm not surprised you have experience of lurid undies!' Victoria jeered. 'You can breathe easily, though, I prefer London, and I intend to go back. Heather can continue to do—whatever she does.'

'She does it very well,' he murmured, his smile growing. 'She has every intention of continuing, even when I marry you.'

Without warning his hands grasped her and pulled her forward, his grip tightening as she pulled uselessly against his strength.

'Victoria with the moonlit hair,' he murmured, his eyes moving over her long fair hair. His grip on her slender shoulders forced her to gaze up at him, and the long silk of her hair fell down her back. 'Beautiful, delicate, decorative, selfish Victoria. Whatever you became in London, I intend to marry you. Andrew's plans suited me fine and he was quite right—I always wanted you. It's not very often that a person can have their cake and eat it too, but you'll never get under my skin, Victoria. I cared deeply about you once. I won't make that mistake twice.'

She struggled wildly, horrified that the cynical voice was getting to her, that the hard, tight hands were still able to seduce her feelings. What did he imagine she had done in London but work all the time to forget her small, unhappy dream? And he had never cared about her. He was busy planning again, but it wasn't going to happen a second time.

'Let me go!' she said coldly, stopping the undignified struggles and glaring into his face.

'Those eyes,' he murmured, 'so green, every green there is—beautiful, impossible eyes, too astonishing to be real. I used to see your face,' he told her, in a suddenly harsh voice. 'Every place that sold magazines seemed to be filled with your image. You looked cold, hard, perfect! Glittering and performing in London for leering men, while your grandfather got older, more lonely. You don't look like that when I hold you, though, you look exactly as you used to look. You're good, aren't you? Everything's a performance.'

'I'm a photographic model. There are no leering men in the studio.'

'There never will be again,' he asserted coldly, not believing her at all, his eyes like blue diamonds, cold and brilliant. 'Don't try to run again, either. You know perfectly well what's going to happen to you. You owe it to Andrew and you owe it to me!'

'You can talk like this, but it's only words. Just how powerful do you imagine you are? I'll do exactly what I want to do!'

'I can talk like this because it's true. The names have always been there and they'll stay. For once in your life you'll face facts. I'll never let those names change, and Kendal and Hunt will never have an outsider!'

'Not even my husband?' Victoria looked up at him scathingly. 'I can marry now, wait until I'm thirty, and then come storming back. All I have to do is keep my own name. That's no hardship—I even like it.'

She turned away and looked out of the window at the names that seemed to dominate the skyline.

'The possibilities are endless,' she mused, a cold delight in her when she realised how much the firm meant to him, how easily she could pay back the years of grief. 'I could bring my husband to all the meetings, make over enough of my shares to him so he could attend board meetings. We could really make our presence felt!'

'You're going to sort through your file of lovers and choose one with a hard enough business-head to face me?' he enquired in sudden amusement.

'Why not?' She spun round to face him, almost flinching as she saw the intense look in those blue eyes. She had expected to see his mockery, but there was none of that. There was a seriously calculating look, a deep speculation.

'Why not?' he murmured. 'Do you think I don't recognise idiotic talk when I hear it? If I thought you even half meant it, Victoria, I would settle all your problems here and now in this quiet house.'

'You'd murder me?' she enquired, her chin tilted proudly.

'No, princess,' he told her softly, 'I'd make you pregnant. An extra Hunt would be a very fine asset.'

'And you imagine I'd be quietly in agreement?' she asked as evenly as she could. Suddenly she was shaking, every limb seemed to be trembling, and she longed to sit down. It was a mixture of shock and memory, memory of times in Damien's arms.

'It would be a pleasure to find out. And I don't think you'd last long. I remember you, Victoria. I remember those soft, clinging arms. Taking you is something I should have done a long time ago. I've always regretted it. Maybe we've reached the appropriate time now.'

'I—I'd kill you!' She felt behind her for a chair and sank down to it, not caring what he thought.

'You wouldn't even try,' he observed cynically. He walked to the door and then turned, his gaze sweeping over her in time to catch the devastated look on her face. 'Destiny, Victoria!' he informed her quietly. 'You are tied to the mills, the names and me. You always were. Now that you'd had your—fling in the big city, you can settle down here and fulfill that destiny. Our children will have a very nice-sounding double-barrelled name, Kendal-Hunt. It has a good ring, don't you think?'

'There'll be no children, because there'll be no marriage!' she managed heatedly, her trembling hands securely in her lap.

'Oh, there'll be children—sooner or later. If you want it to be sooner, just go on talking in that idiotic way— I was never long on patience.'

'You've been quite content to be patient for six years!' She closed her mouth tightly as she heard the slight thread of anguish in her accusation, but apparently he didn't hear it.

'Patience wasn't required,' he informed her ironically. 'I explained to you that I already knew about the will. As to female companionship, I have it already, as you know. That we're both bound by the same destiny is neither here nor there. It's just a fact of life which I accept. I suggest you do the same.'

He just walked out, leaving her staring at the blank face of the door, her head out of time with her heart, the cold matter-of-fact sound of his voice ringing in her ears, the picture his words painted like a grey blanket that stretched on forever, without love, without joy, without pity.

Victoria was still very shaken as she sat later in her hotel bedroom. She had understood all this long ago, but she had never understood the depth of feeling that bound Damien to the valley and the mills. It was not enough that he had things his own way for now, it had to be forever. There was, after all, little difference between Damien and her grandfather.

The names, if they were still so important to him, were his to manoeuvre as he wished. Nobody could stop him from keeping things as they were, or from altering the form of the names that blazed across the valley. He could call his mill anything he desired and there would be no word against him, least of all her own; she would even sell to him to get herself out of this mess, to put sufficient distance between them for any stirring of her heart to be stilled. Apparently it was not enough. He needed a real Kendal permanently. He intended to collect her too! He wanted children with the same names. She found it difficult to believe in this day and age. It was like a throw-back to early Victorian times.

One thing she knew with certainty—she had to get away from here as fast as possible. Today he had simply let her go and walked out of the house, but she had recognised her own weakness as he held her. The memory of being eighteen was not, after all, so very far away, and no one else since had beguiled her as Damien had. Tomorrow she would see the agent and begin to put the sales into action.

She was tired, realising how much these few days had drained her resilience. Sleep would have been a good idea, but on the way back to the hotel she had seen Jeremy Lloyd, and when he waved her down she had allowed herself to be talked into having dinner with him. She regretted it. It had merely been an act of defiance against Damien, as most of her rebellion in life had been to defy him. He wouldn't even know, and now she was safely out of his reach it seemed stupid.

She was committed, however, and as the time drew close she began to get ready with little enthusiasm, realising perfectly well that she was being slow. She had the decided feeling that Jeremy would prove to be a bore—that he had always been a bore, but she had been too young to recognise the fact. She wished heartily that Joel was at home. She could talk to Joel.

A knock on her door irritated her further, and she glanced at her watch. It was only just seven-thirty—surely Jeremy had understood when she had said eight? If he was now pounding on her door, it showed exactly what a nuisance he had become since she had last known him. She wasn't even dressed yet!

She opened the door with a rather grim expression on her face, and stopped in surprise that bordered on shock to see Damien standing there, looking exceptionally pleased with himself.

'What do you want?'

Self-defence was automatic with Damien, and he grinned as if he knew it was exactly that. He then stepped inside, after lifting her easily out of his way, his strong hands on her slender waist. Since she had seen him earlier his whole manner seemed to have changed. He was simply amused, no anger or threat was there.

'I'm trying to calculate exactly how many times you've greeted me with similar words since I saw you again,' he said thoughtfully. 'You have a collection of well-learned phrases?'

'It was merely an astonished question!' Victoria snapped. 'I didn't expect to be accosted in my hotel bedroom. I have a dinner-date.'

'Lloyd? I know,' he murmured, walking in and looking round with interest. 'He was downstairs when I came in. He looked so agitated that I noticed him at once. I've sent him about his business.'

'You've what?' Victoria's eyes turned a very dark green, and he looked down at her in amusement, her growing rage merely bringing a twinkle to the blue eyes.

'I'll rephrase that, as you don't understand. I sent him packing. He was early, as he told me. He looked uncomfortably eager. I told him I had to talk to you urgently—business. Of course he understood. He'll ring you tomorrow.'

'And I'll talk any business that's necessary tomorrow!' Victoria said sharply. 'I have to see the agent about selling the house and contents. I can spare a few minutes for you at about ten-thirty.' She tossed her head defiantly and he smiled at her.

'I don't want to talk business, sweetie,' he said softly, his arms shooting out and capturing her by the waist. 'I came to take you down to dinner. As Lloyd had beat me to it, I despatched him rapidly.'

'And he let you!' Through the thin material of her robe his hand was warm and tempting; she spun away, biting into her lips when she realised that she had wanted him to go on holding her. It was sheer madness.

'Not everyone has your fighting spirit. He has an eye to the main chance in any case,' Damien murmured, leaning back against the door and eyeing her appreciatively. 'Heather is in my office. I think her brother hopes I'll become fatally interested. I'd make a useful brother-in-law, after all.'

'You may make whatever you want, just so long as it doesn't concern me at all!'

He smiled that cool smile she had dreaded.

'I expected you to be almost ready. I certainly expected you to be dressed,' he murmured, his lips quirking. 'Models are supposed to be very slick at changing, aren't they? Still, I imagine you're quite used to having men wait while you drift around in your négligé.'

'All the time!' Victoria snapped. 'I never hesitated to answer the door.' She went perfectly still and looked up at him as pointedly as she could, realising immediately that it was a mistake—a big one.

'I noticed!'

His own face was still too, and the blue eyes were dangerously narrowed, the humour quite gone. Defiance with Damien should definitely be conducted at a distance. She tried to move stealthily away, but his arm shot out and captured her, his grip tightening as she struggled.

'I'll see you tomorrow, Damien,' she said uneasily.

'You'll see me tonight!' he countered. 'Dinner in fifteen minutes, or we conduct our business right here and now.'

'I don't want to have dinner with you!' she informed him fretfully, trying again to step free, and he pulled her into his arms, looking down at her with brilliant, narrowed eyes.

'I'm not particularly interested in dinner, either,' he murmured quietly. 'It's more private here for the discussion I have in mind. We'll stay here.'

He pulled her close. He was still leaning against the door and she found herself moulded to his strength as his arms came tightly around her.

'I—I know why you're doing this!' she said frantically. 'You're trying to force me to—to——'

'I won't have to force you,' he taunted softly, his hand capturing her wildly moving head. 'You never needed forcing, once you got the general idea. In fact, you surprised me. I had no notion you were so eager. You've had plenty of practice since then. I'm very anxious to find out how much.'

CHAPTER FIVE

VICTORIA struggled wildly, and Damien looked down at her with amusement.

'Why the terrified act? You've been in this situation plenty of times since I last knew you. Maybe you would have been here later with Lloyd, if I hadn't got rid of him. At least with me it's an honourable situation, as we're about to be married.'

Always he had attacked her. Always he had delivered blows to her self-esteem. Except for the magical year when she had grown from seventeen to eighteen, and he had almost seemed to be guarding her affectionately, he had scorned her for no reason whatsoever.

She clawed at him, coming to vibrant, angry life, her breath angry sobs in her throat, her hands beating against his chest, her body moving violently, until he crushed her against him, his fingers twisting into her hair, tightening cruelly.

It stopped her, and she looked up at him. It was tragic, because he was still the same. The scent of him was the same in her nostrils, his warmth was the same, and the lost years came back with all their loneliness and anxiety.

'Let me go, Damien.'

She didn't care if he heard the pleading in her voice. He had heard it before. He had haunted her dreams since she was little more than a child. He had walked like a god through her world, a destiny she had recognised without even knowing it. There was no resistance in her when Damien was near, even though she knew the reason for this. All she could do was shout and fight, hoping to keep him at a distance.

'Please, let me go,' she begged.

His hand released her hair, his eyes following the contours of her face.

'I don't intend to, because whatever future you have, I'm in it. Don't bother to beg to be free. You never have been free. You've always been for me, and now it's collecting time.'

'We—we could have a business deal—an arrangement, Damien.'

'A business arrangement? Oh, yes, Victoria, we'll have that. Business partners and partners in bed. Even if children *weren't* needed, I couldn't keep my hands off you. I don't intend to try.'

He forced her head to his, claiming her lips determinedly, taking her breath away, and she didn't struggle for long—she couldn't, not with Damien. She was back in time, yearning against him, and he moved to accept her, his legs parting to bring her closer.

Her arms wound around his neck and she stopped thinking altogether. There was no thinking when Damien held her; there was only feeling, wonderful, breathtaking feeling. She was leaning softly against him, and he groaned deep in his throat, his hand sliding down her back to pull her against the aroused strength of his body.

She was back in his arms, the years gone as if they had never existed, feeling too young again, the arms of the most powerful man in the world around her. He had always been that to her, since she was only a child, and she forgot everything else in between.

Everything was going out of control. They were kissing each other like passionate enemies, devouring each other, and Damien swept her up and lowered her to the bed, his mouth not leaving hers for a minute.

'You want me,' he breathed into her mouth, 'and, hell, I want you!'

She wasn't content to listen—his lips had lifted from hers, and she searched for them with anxious little cries until he crushed her close again, and came back to her. It was heaven to feel his touch, to feel his hands shaping her body, and she sighed against his lips.

Her breath came in short, uneven gasps and she looked at him with wide, mesmerised eyes. He smiled slowly and ran his fingers down her spine, and she gasped, moulding herself to him as if she was meant to be there.

'Born for me,' he said huskily. 'Made for no other purpose.' His hand opened, drawing her tightly to his hips, leaving her in no doubt of his desire, and she was seared with flame. Shamelessly she murmured against his skin, her lips searching his face now, her tiny moans of pleasure bringing a satisfied sound from deep in his throat.

'Damien!'

Even to her own ears her voice sounded abandoned, so filled with yearning that there would be no pretending later that this had not happened, and with a deep groan of male pleasure his mouth closed over hers, probing and searching, his hands sensuous and possessive, parting her négligé to move beneath the lace of her slip and close over the silken thrust of her breast.

His head bent to capture the tight, hard peak and she began to move wildly, her whole body trembling and alive as he moved over her demandingly. He struggled out of his jacket, and the shock of his movement brought her partly to reality, his words of this afternoon ringing hazily in her mind. He was bringing her to heel so easily. All part of the glorious master plan. Tears filled her eyes, and her aching body began to shake with silent sobbing.

It was just like before—a great pretence.

'Victoria?' His hand lifted her face and he saw the tears streaming down it. 'So! You're not quite so willing when the chips are down?' he asked harshly, his breathing thick and heavy. 'You've had plenty of experience, though, haven't you? That was no great act! What do they do? Come and collect you after work? Is there a rota?'

She couldn't believe the cold cruelty, and she stared at him through her tears.

'You pig!'

'Am I?' he asked tightly. 'And what are you, Victoria? I'll admit to getting more than I bargained for, but let's say your experience took my breath away.'

He stood and looked down at her, as she hastily drew her wrap tightly to her.

'Get dressed and come down to dinner!' he snapped, his breathing still unsteady.

'There's no way that I'll——' she began, the tears still on her face.

'If you're not there in reasonable time, I'll come back for you,' he threatened, 'and this time I'll not stop!' He walked to the door and looked round. 'And it won't mean a damned thing to me, either, except male satisfaction and the chance to settle your future swiftly!'

He slammed the door as he left, and she lay there miserable and dazed, too shaken to move. She still felt the same about him. Her feelings left nothing to the imagination. It was like a battle to the death, hating and loving wildly, but with Damien there was nothing but determination and she could never let him win. It would be the end of her.

She knew she could never recover with Damien's remarkable speed, but she tried to still the wild beating of her heart and get ready. If she lingered he would come back and subdue her again in a similar manner, and this

time he would go much further. He had probed and
found her weakness and he would not hesitate.

Her days of defying Damien were over; escape was
the only solution. He had seen behind the icy calm, and
discovered that she was merely a little older. She was no
wiser than she had ever been, and he knew it.

He greeted her as if nothing had happened, his eyes
quickly scanning her face. She had herself under tight
control now, and he smiled derisively at her cool, calm
look.

'Years of practice. Congratulations. I wonder how
long it would have taken you to get back into that cold
shell if I'd stayed?'

'I wouldn't have allowed you to stay,' she said tightly.
'You don't own everything in this valley. You don't own
this hotel.'

'I own you,' he pointed out softly, his hand catching
hers across the table. 'I may not own you physically yet,
but I'm right there in your mind, waiting.'

'The King of the Castle!' she said scornfully, her face
flushed at his words.

'The king of *your* castle, princess!' he assured her
sardonically.

He never asked what she wanted to eat, he simply ordered, and she was not yet so smoothly controlled that
she could protest. The wine helped, but not all that
much—any assistance from that was more than cancelled out by the thoughtful eyes that watched her so
intently.

'Tomorrow I'll take you round the works,' he told her
quietly as they ate, and, as the food was already threatening to choke her, she put down her knife and fork and
looked at him as steadily as she could. Why shouldn't
she face him, after all? She had been in his arms before,
rendered mindless and pleading. He excelled at it. It was
no surprise to him. Plenty of other women must have

given him the same satisfying flip to his ego. Heather did it regularly!

'Tomorrow, I'm seeing the agent, visiting Molly and settling my affairs here. If everything is completed then, I'll leave the next day.'

'One day, the mills will be partly yours,' he reminded her, his manner quite astonishingly reasonable in view of his threats. 'Whatever happens in the meantime, whatever happens between us, one thing remains true; you are Victoria Kendal, and the mills are yours as well as Joel's and mine. Any reasonable person would realise how short a time six years is in the business world. To my certain knowledge, you were never allowed in there. Andrew's will seems a little more sensible when your attitude is searched closely. You're an heiress to a large and thriving business, you have a name that is well-loved and respected in these parts. It will not reflect too well on Andrew's memory if his granddaughter merely wishes to walk off with the loot. Andrew used to go round and talk to the people, he knew about every problem they had. They'll think he brought you up to simply queen it over them, and everything he ever did for them will be swamped in the knowledge that it was all just a sham.'

Memories flooded her mind, memories of people coming to the house, her grandfather greeting them like old friends, talking to them for hours to iron out problems that were nothing at all to do with the mills. This was a tightly knit community, a small kingdom surrounded by inhospitable moorland. Everyone needed each other here.

Other memories raced forward too: her grandfather's wry sense of humour, his reassuring arms, his laughter. He had still been like that when he had come to London to see her, his booming laugh bringing smiles to faces that would normally have been irritated when she had taken him to see a show. She had kept every one of his letters; they were full of love, even though it was never spoken. She had never been able to blame him for his old-fashioned ideas. After her hurt and anger, she had simply blamed Damien. How could she allow people to think ill of her grandfather?

She looked up, and the brilliant blue eyes were watching her intently.

'Damn you, Damien!' she muttered angrily, trapped as she had once felt trapped before, but with no ability now to run.

'I'll take you round the works straight after you've seen the agent,' he said quietly, pouring her some more wine. 'Eat your dinner, there are several pairs of curious eyes on us.'

'And I must remember that I'm a Kendal,' she fumed quietly, beginning to eat again after one sharp glance round had assured her that he was speaking the truth.

'Temporarily,' he conceded, his brilliant glance shooting up to alarm her all over again. 'We'll take things slowly, though, if you're prepared to be reasonable. One thing at a time. Tomorrow, the works; after that, we'll see.'

'I'm going for Grandfather, and for no other reason,' she said in a low, angry voice.

'Then, if you've finally remembered Andrew, remember that he expected the two names to combine. He also expected it to be legal.' His eyes held hers and he suddenly smiled, that long, seductive smile that could raise her temperature in seconds. 'Eat your dinner, princess,' he advised gently. 'I wouldn't want you to lose weight. At the moment you're perfect. I like my women tall and slender.'

'Poor Heather!' Victoria snapped thoughtlessly.

'There's no need to worry,' he remarked sardonically. 'I'm bound to offer the ring to you, as you know perfectly well.'

'My desire to keep grandfather's name bright does not extend to martyrdom!' She glared at him, and to her surprise, he laughed delightedly and said nothing at all.

By the next day, a great deal of Victoria's determination to get rid of the house had simply faded away. She somehow felt she did not have the right. It might be hers now, but she should surely hold it in trust for the generations who would come after her, just as it had been held in trust for her. She arrived early, the new and uncomfortable ideas swimming in her mind. What was wrong with her? She had decided exactly what she was going to do, even before she had come back to this place. The only difference now would be that there would be a delay before she inherited everything—a long delay.

She walked around the house with a notebook, pencil poised to determine which of the old pieces she was going to keep for herself, but after a very little while she realised she could not decide at all—they were not hers to sell, they seemed to stand there chastising her, and she walked to the phone, cancelling her appointment with the agent.

It gave her plenty of time to get ready for meeting with Damien, and she was waiting for him when he walked into the hotel. There was no way he was going to get up to her room again.

'Nice and early?' He looked at her quizzically. 'Does this denote eagerness?'

'When I have to face something unpleasant, I like to get it over with,' Victoria informed him coolly. 'I suggest we go now.'

The brilliant blue eyes lanced over her, his smile sardonic as he noted the blue suit and crisp white blouse.

'The executive image? Six years too soon, unless you decide to come to your senses,' he taunted. 'Today you're merely showing the flag.'

'And you know exactly why.'

'I know exactly why,' he acknowledged, leading her out to his car.

She was stiffly silent, but it didn't seem to bother him at all.

'You were very quick with the agent,' he remarked, as they left the hotel and drove towards the mills. 'I called there expecting to have to pick you up, but the whole place was locked and barred.'

'I cancelled the whole thing.' She turned her face away, her hands clasped tightly in her lap, willing him to mind his own business, but, of course, he didn't.

'Ah! You've discovered a conscience?'

'I simply can't make my mind up which pieces of furniture to keep.' She turned on him angrily. 'As for calling for me there, I had already arranged to meet you here, and you can stop checking on my activities. I have nothing to do with you, except that in six years' time we'll be business partners—until I sell!'

'We'll be partners well before then,' he murmured. 'I can't wait for such a long, dreary time. Life, as they say, is passing me by. The whole valley is waiting to see what happens next. They know perfectly well that you've inherited, except that they assume you've inherited at once. People can't be kept on tenterhooks for six years. It's their livelihood. Besides, a situation like this leaves us very vulnerable. We don't want the wolves around.'

'What do you mean? There are other wolves besides you?' Victoria looked at him scathingly, and received a slanting glance from the piercing eyes, a glance that was all amusement.

'I imagine so, but the wolves I'm thinking of will have take-over on their minds. This is a prosperous business, but the first thing a take-over does is rationalise and ensure redundancies. The valley is therefore uneasy. People want to know what's happening.'

'We're too wealthy to be gobbled up,' Victoria scorned, 'so you can stop trying to frighten me.'

'We wouldn't stand a chance against a big corporation,' Damien sighed, with an exasperation that, for once, didn't irritate her.

'Do you really think——'

'I'm not trying to think at all on that particular score,' Damien assured her grimly.

'They couldn't hurt you, Damien, could they? I mean, you're too wealthy in your own right—mills apart?'

He gave her a long, considering glance, and it was only then she realised that she had shown concern for him—a personal concern.

'I diversified a long time ago,' he said, 'but, if the worst came to the worst, I would put it all on the line for Kendal and Hunt.'

'But why?' She stared at his handsome profile and he never looked round.

'I care. Therefore I want our affairs settled, and the wolves from the door.'

'You're making all this utterly impossible!' She turned away again, determined not to be dragged into things. 'You don't even know if anyone is interested.'

'Instinct. Business instinct. The baleful eye is easy to recognise when you've been in things as long as I have. I was wheeling and dealing when you were a tender babe. In any case,' he added evenly, 'I want you. It's not all business.'

'You don't care about me!' she blazed, hurt by his attitude.

'I don't have to care about you to want you,' he explained, with infuriating and wounding calm. 'You wiped out the tenderness. On a purely physical basis, though, you're desirable. It makes a business marriage acceptable.'

'Not to me!'

He shrugged elegantly.

'You're already partly boxed in. I've dealt with more difficult problems.

'I'm not boxed in at all!'

'You want me. We're half-way there. Time is on my side, but not too much of it, as I've just explained. I can afford to let you run loose for no more than a few weeks. Action will soon be called for.'

'You're not frightening me, Damien,' she assured him, as coolly as possible.

'Frightening you? I'm explaining, princess, as if you were a person with intelligence.'

He became silent, and gradually her heart returned to a more normal beat. The mills came in sight, and he swung off the road to go through the big iron gates that had been there since the mills were first built by their great-great-grandfathers.

They wouldn't have recognised the place now though, Victoria thought, as the car swung down the long drive to the old, handsome buildings that sat securely in the lower reaches of the valley, the river's bend cutting close to the side. This was no dirty old decaying structure. Every bit of it had been restored and modernised. The great bolts of cloth were taken away from the back, and the entrance was as smart and pleasing as the approach to many old country houses.

Lawns stretched from the higher road down to the factory walls, the borders bright with flowers, and as the car swept under an arch that had stood unchanged since the Industrial Revolution Victoria's heart returned to an uneven pounding. She was quite out of her depth, relying solely on Damien.

'I've never been here before,' she murmured, with just a touch of anxiety in her voice. 'Grandfather wouldn't let me.' She didn't want to speak to him, but she had to. He was suddenly a sort of refuge.

'You had a certain disadvantage,' Damien reminded her quietly, taking her arm and leading her to the tall door below the arch. 'You were a girl.'

'But I should have been here. I should have been allowed to come. Joel came while we were still at school. You came and took over.'

'Nobody ever mistook me for a girl,' Damien said drily. 'Naturally, we *had* to come. We were expected to work here, to get to know everything, to understand our obligations and our inheritance.'

'It's my inheritance too!' Victoria said sharply.

'And your obligation!' he reminded her just as sharply, turning her to face him. 'That, after all, is why we're here today—to see what belongs to you, and to face the responsibilities that you now share. Andrew was locked in another time sphere, and he locked you out of any modern outlook as far as Kendal and Hunt were concerned. Now you're in, and you can face your destiny like a Kendal. Your days of being a delicate object to be admired and not touched are over.'

'I've never been that!' Her angry, defensive voice merely tightened his lips further.

'I can well imagine! We'll not linger on the subject of not being touched. Admiration is earned here— beautiful faces and desirable bodies don't count.'

'Except with you!' she bit out unwisely, her face flushing as he stared down at her intently.

'I tend to collect what is mine,' he informed her, 'even though the goods have been looked over and handled.'

'I don't have to listen to this, not even for Grandfather!' She stopped and pulled angrily away from his hand, her face flushed with embarrassment and annoyance.

'Provoke me and I'll punish you,' he said acidly, 'even when we're married! I see no reason to treat you like a tender young thing any more.'

'You never did. I hate you, Damien.'

'Hate away,' he taunted softly. 'If you fight me on our wedding night, it will merely add spice to the surrender.'

'You know I'm not going to marry you,' she said quietly, turning away.

He was beginning to get through the barrier of distrust she had built. It was not easy to stand up to it. Her grandfather's ways had been indulgent in many things, and she had never doubted his love, but there had been suppression there too. She had fought for every small right she had ever achieved. Damien's only thought now, *and* before, had been to take over and continue the suppression.

'If you can control the urge to sulk,' he mocked, 'we'll continue.'

It wasn't worth the effort to answer back, and she didn't. She walked on and stared straight ahead, stiffening up to face things as she had always had to. It was not her heritage. It had never felt like that. It was a tight band that held her fast, and she regretted her sentimental action this morning. When this minor ordeal was over, she would telephone the agent and tell him to collect her keys. He could catalogue everything and sell the lot. She didn't want any pieces of furniture from the house. They would only be a reminder of the chains that tried to hold her—a reminder of Damien.

The whole place was too much for her. It spoke of her grandfather and distant forebears, whose portraits hung in the old house: bewhiskered men with determined faces, men who towered over subdued-looking women. It spoke of powerful men with clever brains and a ruthless way of winning, men like Damien, who was not even content with this small empire, but had built another.

'My destiny doesn't rest here,' she said quietly.

His eyes narrowed on her rather frantic face.

'It rests with me,' he said softly, 'and there's nothing to be afraid of, Victoria. It's only the same destiny you ran away from six years ago. If you run again, it will still be here, waiting.'

'Why?' She looked up at him a little desperately, and his hand touched her face lightly.

'It has to be,' he said simply.

It sounded like a trap that was fast closing around her, but she didn't attempt to pull away from his guiding hand again. His voice had held a little tragedy of its own then. If he believed all this about the mills, the valley and their great obligation, then wasn't Damien trapped too? Perhaps he didn't want to marry her at all really?

'We don't have to be tied into this, Damien,' she said softly.

'Then perhaps we should never have been born. As we were born, and as we bear the names, we *are* tied into it.'

He just walked quietly on, and she knew it was no use speaking about it again. She even wondered why she had bothered. He was just as intransigent as her grandfather.

She was quite lost here, not just an interested visitor, but an object of interest. She would need plenty of nerve to survive it. The icy shutters came down over her face, the same shutters that had allowed her to cloak her shyness and bewilderment when she had first gone to London. They would do as well as anything.

Damien glanced at her, and his expression tightened as he saw her cold indifference. Let him think what he liked. She just wanted to get it over and done with, then she would escape. She would escape tomorrow, or the next day at the latest.

In spite of her fears, she became fascinated. Whatever anyone thought, they were polite and pleasant, and she knew that it was not solely because Damien was with her every step of the way; they were hard-working, polite people, kindliness was in their bloodstream, and they remembered her grandfather.

There was noise, but not the level of noise she had expected. Most of the noise seemed to be coming from the music that was being played all the time, not from the smoothly moving machines. Damien was working as he conducted her around, stopping to chat to the foreman, to sign order forms, to listen to problems. He was involved in a deep discussion about one of the machines with a group of men when a bell rang loudly, and everything stopped.

Damien and his group simply continued, tools were out, and Damien was actually on his knees beside a giant machine when Victoria found a steaming mug of tea thrust into her hand.

'Tea-break!'

She looked round to find a middle-aged woman smiling at her, with no sign of the disapproval she had expected.

'Get yours now, while it's hot, love. The men just keep right on going when they've got their heads into one of those machines. Mr Hunt is as bad as they are.'

'Oh, thank you.'

She felt a little lost, but it didn't last long. The others drifted over towards her, their tea in their hands and a great deal of inquisitiveness in their eyes. Victoria didn't know what to say, but it was all taken out of her hands very easily. Gossip was a way of life with these women.

'You're a model, aren't you?' One of the younger girls looked at Victoria with great interest, and Victoria nodded a trifle self-consciously, wondering what was coming next.

'I bet it's thrilling, glamorous!'

'Not really,' Victoria said. 'It's hard work and often boring—cold sometimes, too,' she added with a grin.

'Getting in and out of all them clothes!' one of the older women observed, and there was general laughter, in which Victoria joined happily.

'I'd love to have a go.'

The girl who had spoken looked at Victoria wistfully, but the laughter grew louder as one woman observed tartly, 'You'd have to lose two stone. No more chocolate, Sandra!'

'You must have felt terrible, not being here when your grandfather died.' There was a strained silence at this remark, and Victoria stiffened. Here it comes, she thought.

'Yes,' she said honestly. 'I didn't see too much of him recently. I'm totally lost here, too. I should have been here right from the first, like Mr Hunt and Joel.'

'Whatever for?'

There was a whole chorus of denial of her quiet self-condemnation.

'You had your own job!'

'It must have been really lonely up in that big old house.'

'Plenty of people would have sat back and done nothing about earning their own living.'

'It gave us all a boost to see one of our own on magazine covers. Every shop sold out straight away!'

'Come in here and have a look.' The woman who had brought her tea grasped Victoria's arm in a grip that would not have disgraced Damien, and Victoria was swept along in a wave of chattering enthusiasm to the rest-room.

The magazine covers had been cut out and stuck on the wall. It stunned her. Rather than envying her, these women were proud of her achievements.

'Kendal and Hunt Fan Club!'

There was a great laugh at this remark and Victoria looked around with interest.

'I bet you get changed in better surroundings than these?' The blonde, slightly overweight girl with the desire to model murmured romantically.

'Not always,' Victoria assured her. 'Then again, I'm only there to change and do my face up; it's not supposed to be a rest-room. This is a trifle barren. I think the words "Ladies Rest-Room" on the door overstate the case a bit. What do you do if you feel off-colour?'

'Sit on a nice hard chair for as long as possible, and then carry on.'

'Does Mr Hunt know what it's like in here?'

'No, and the foreman being a man, what can you expect?'

'Well, doesn't Mr Hunt's secretary come and take a look?'

The sudden silence was broken rather angrily by the would-be model. 'Not Miss Lloyd! She doesn't look further than Mr Hunt.'

Everyone began to talk at once in an embarrassed flurry of sound, and Victoria stifled the sudden stab of feeling that shot through her.

'I'll speak to him myself.'

There was the sound of the bell again, and all the tea was finished in a rush as the tea break ended. Victoria walked out in the middle of the chattering, smiling little group to meet the astonished blue eyes of Damien, as he stood waiting for her with a slightly bemused expression on his face.

CHAPTER SIX

'THEY didn't beat you up, then?' Damien murmured, as they left the floor and went up to his office.

'No. They were quite pleased to be able to talk to a woman. What percentage of women work here?'

'About thirty per cent are women at the moment,' he told her, with a quick look at her thoughtful face as he opened his office door, motioning her inside. 'Any reason for asking?'

'I merely wondered who looks after their interests?'

'I do, or Joel.' He looked at her steadily, and Victoria looked back.

'Do you inspect their rest-room?'

'Of course I don't!' He looked a bit hot under the collar and she smiled sweetly.

'Then maybe you should appoint a woman to supervise their needs. I suggest the one who brought me my tea; I believe she's called Ava. She's got a grip to match yours,' she added, moving her arm from his grasp. 'Maybe you could do some arm wrestling with her.'

'You're sticking your oar in immediately?' he murmured with wry amusement.

'I thought I was fulfilling my obligations and my destiny,' she informed him, with a wide-eyed look of innocence. 'It seemed like a good place to start. Small beginnings, you know?'

'You've got a destiny that's a great deal more interesting than a Ladies Rest-Room,' he growled, looking at her intently, the blue eyes vivid on her flushed face.

'Interesting to you, perhaps!' Victoria snapped under her breath, suddenly becoming aware that they were not alone.

'Tell me that the day after the wedding,' he taunted, his smile still wry, as he turned to look at the woman who stood with tight lips by his desk. 'Did you get the mail out, Heather?' he asked pleasantly, and the atmosphere warmed just a little as he smiled across at Heather Lloyd, who relaxed almost visibly.

'Of course, Damien.' She smiled at him in an altogether sultry manner, and then turned cold eyes on Victoria. 'Why, Victoria! You're a complete stranger nowadays.'

'I've always been a little strange,' Victoria said drily. 'However, I won't be here long enough for anyone to notice. I'm going back to London tomorrow or the day after.'

'She's just going to be here long enough to interfere a little,' Damien remarked. 'Get me the file on Ava Hastings, will you?'

'Yes, Damien.' She left hurriedly after one more sultry glance at him, and Victoria stifled the sharp stab of pain that had come when he had readily accepted that she would go back. Now that she had seen how he and Heather looked at each other, she didn't wonder at it.

His reaction as the door shut, therefore, took her completely off guard.

'I've told you that you're going nowhere!' he grated. 'In three weeks you'll be a very married lady, and you'll live right here. Any rumours you start about going will only unsettle people more.'

'I'm to be dragged screaming to the altar?' Victoria asked angrily. 'Heather didn't look too unsettled. It seemed to restore her balance!'

'She's not yet decided whether to be jealous or not,' he explained mockingly, the anger draining as quickly

as it had come. 'And don't worry about the wedding, I'll prepare you the night before.' His eyes ran over the beautiful length of her legs as she sat down. 'If Heather wasn't here, I'd start right now. We could continue where we left off last night. There's a nice long settee in this room.'

'I noticed. I've got it earmarked for the Ladies Rest-Room. What could you possibly want with a thing like that in here?' she added, her eyes going deliberately to the door that had closed behind Heather Lloyd.

She had a sudden urge to goad him—a purely sexual urge, she realised. It was like playing with fire, pushing him to see when she would be burned.

He smiled slowly, his eyes running over her figure.

'Heather?' he murmured softly. 'We don't use the office. It wouldn't be suitable, with Joel in and out all day long, and the pictures of the ancestors looking down in annoyance.'

'You're disgusting!' Victoria stood abruptly, her face flushed, wishing she had not brought this up at all. She didn't want to even think of Heather with him. She was jealous!

The force of his aggressive masculinity seemed to lash out and surround her.

'Perhaps,' he said acidly, his eyes sweeping over her. 'But then, I don't pretend. Everything is out in the open with me, and Heather has never been one to act bashfully. *You*, though, Victoria, still act like a princess and try to deny the life you lead in the big city.'

'Let's both act exactly as we like, shall we?' Victoria asked, tired of denying things to Damien. 'We are, after all, nothing but future business partners, and even that's not going to last. I'm here today to show the flag, as you pointed out. I'll do this one thing to show willing, and then I'll be on my way, back to my—friends.'

Damien's expression made Victoria greatly relieved to see the door open and Heather Lloyd come back into the room, a file in her hand. She even managed to look slinky in a skirt and blouse, Victoria noticed, and she had a few too many curves. The additional rather spiteful thought brought a slight smile to her lips as she looked at Heather, and Damien's dark brows drew together in a tight frown.

'Look this over and let me know what you think of her for the job!' he grated, tossing the file to Victoria. There was nothing mocking about him now, and Victoria felt a moment of triumph that she had been able to get under his skin a little. Let him believe exactly what he wanted to believe. He had left her with no illusions about himself and Heather. Joel was right about them. And he *dared* to demand that she marry him!

'Is Mrs Hastings being promoted?' Heather asked sharply, annoyed, no doubt, that she hadn't been consulted.

'It all depends on the boss-lady,' Damien informed her sourly. 'We'll need an extra office here too, I suppose,' he added, with an irritated glance at Victoria.

'I'll share this one with you,' Victoria offered pleasantly, not knowing whether to laugh or cry as Heather blushed and looked anxiously at Damien.

'That sounds like a good idea,' he countered silkily, his eyes moving deliberately from her slender figure to the settee. 'We'll deal with the rest-room problem and then get around to that.'

She opened the file rapidly, and looked at it with a deep interest she didn't feel, berating herself for trying her hand at goading Damien. He held all the aces, and the sooner she took to her heels the better.

Damien left the office and she read through the file, trying to keep her mind on it, quite sure that Damien would question her like a child facing a stiff test. She had almost got to the stage of being absorbed in Ava Hastings's home details, when Heather walked in.

'Have you finished with that file?'

'Almost. Damien is going to want it, though.' Victoria looked up and met the full blaze of antagonism.

'It's going to be very difficult if you try to alter things here, Victoria,' Heather said stiffly. 'Damien has this place exactly as he wants it. You'll not find it easy to come here throwing your weight about.'

'I have no such intention,' Victoria said calmly. 'I don't have the greatest interest in this place. You do realise that I live and work in London? I'm not likely to be here for much longer.'

'Damien was talking as if you were going to stay,' Heather said, in a more friendly tone.

'His little joke, no doubt?' Victoria enquired pleasantly.

She was finding it surprisingly difficult to speak to Heather Lloyd. It had been a good deal easier to talk to the women in the mill. The thought came back into her mind that she was jealous, but she crushed it before it could take on a threatening shape. She would never be able to be with Damien, and he didn't care about her. She doubted if he cared about anything other than the future of this old firm.

'I'll have to ask him about it the next time he takes me out,' Heather murmured with a little laugh, utterly coy.

'Do!' Victoria looked at her steadily and then stood, picking up her bag and preparing to leave. 'I'm really surprised to see you working here, Heather,' she said quietly, horrified to find that she was probing into Heather's motives with an almost morbid desire to know how things stood between Heather and Damien.

'Oh, well, Damien asked me, and you know how I've always felt about Damien. I've been after him since I was seventeen.'

And before that! Victoria thought, with a bitterness that frightened her.

Damien walked in, his eyes alert as he saw them talking.

'I'll take you back now, Victoria,' he offered quietly. 'We'll discuss the new appointment tonight over dinner.'

'I'm having dinner with Jeremy tonight,' Victoria said promptly. 'I just can't disappoint him twice, and I did have dinner with you last night.'

She just couldn't help saying that to make Heather take notice, and Damien was amused at once. He watched her beautiful, swinging walk, the long elegance of her legs, his eyes on her with no thought of Heather's furious face. He didn't even glance across to say goodbye to his hopeful secretary; instead the hand came back in that tight, possessive grip that Victoria was beginning to dread, and he shut the door to his office and turned her to the steps.

'Heather will be jealous,' she said sweetly.

'Not for long. When I've dropped you off I'm coming back here, don't forget. Keep your dinner date,' he finished quietly, 'but see that he doesn't end up in your room. We know what happens there, but from now on it only happens with me!'

As she had suspected, Jeremy Lloyd was a bore—she found that out even before the pre-dinner drinks were finished, and she was glad that she had insisted upon dining in the hotel where she was staying. It would be easier to plead tiredness and go to bed. They had not even moved to their table before Heather walked in, and Victoria's heart leapt alarmingly and then sank as Damien walked in slightly behind her. She was shocked to find how much it hurt to see them together. She must be going quite mad here, and there was no future in it—there never had been.

'How astonishing!' Damien smiled slowly, that taunting smile that alarmed and infuriated her. 'I imagined you'd be dining elsewhere.'

'I wanted to, but Victoria insisted upon staying here,' Jeremy said quickly, like a schoolboy caught out in some sordid little trick. Damien had that effect on everyone. Victoria glared at him.

'We may as well join forces then,' Damien suggested smoothly and, to Victoria's chagrin, Jeremy nodded like some half-witted puppet, and signalled the waiter to set their table for four.

'Does everyone shiver when you speak?' she muttered angrily, as Heather was momentarily engaged in conversation with an acquaintance and Jeremy was instructing the waiter.

'Possibly. I don't expect it, though. I'm more than content if a slight shiver touches your spine,' he mocked softly.

'I'm made of slightly sterner stuff!' Victoria snapped, her voice low and angry. There had been a shiver down her spine when she had seen him walk in; there was a shiver now, and it wasn't fear either.

'You don't look at all the sturdy type. You never did. A beautiful butterfly, gauzy and delicate, waiting to nestle in the palm of my hand.' His hand captured her wrist, his long fingers immediately on her racing pulse. 'Excitement?' he tormented.

'Rage!' She pulled free and turned a brilliant smile on Jeremy that had his face bright with embarrassed pleasure at once.

It was not the best meal she had ever had, Victoria mused, as they sat through each course steadfastly. The food might have been excellent, but she really didn't notice. The conversation was stilted, only Damien at his ease, and he watched her with cruel intensity until she simply sat silently and looked around the huge room at the other guests. The place seemed to be filled with Americans, tourists who had come over to see the Brontë country and settled themselves in the best hotel for miles around. Victoria shamelessly eavesdropped, and she was startled into awareness of her own party when she realised that Damien was speaking to her, and that his words had wiped the last of the smug smile from Heather's face.

'I'm sorry? I didn't——'

'I said that I haven't danced with you since you were eighteen,' Damien repeated amusedly. 'I asked you to dance.'

For a moment she looked wildly to Jeremy for support, but he was talking a little desperately to his sister and there was no way out. She stood unwillingly, and Damien came to pull her seat back and lead her out to the floor.

'What a very acceptable escort you have,' he taunted quietly. 'I quite approve of the arrangement until we're engaged. He knows exactly when to give in.'

'Like all the time when you're here!' Victoria muttered angrily. 'Why are you doing this?'

'You know perfectly well why,' he assured her softly, his arms closing around her. 'I want you in my arms. This is the only decent way I can go about it at the moment.' His head lowered and his lips brushed her ear. 'We could ask them to excuse us, though—I'm sure that Lloyd would be willing to take Heather home this once, and I could come discreetly to your room.'

She pulled away furiously, but only succeeded in gaining a few inches.

'Are you trying to make me hate you more?' she raged quietly, every nerve alert to him.

'How could you?' he enquired smoothly. 'As I recall, you've had an abiding hatred for me all your life. I'm not exactly filled with admiration for your character either.'

'Then, taking the two factors into consideration, lead me back to the table and in future keep your distance!' Victoria snapped.

'Impossible,' he said with taunting regret. 'We have to marry and, as I keep pointing out, I want you. I'm prepared to overlook your failings for the pleasure of owning you, body and soul.'

'For the pleasure of owning all Kendal and Hunt!' she reminded him, her heart racing almost audibly.

'But I *do* own all of Kendal and Hunt,' he said silkily, 'at least for the next six years, and then you're going to sell to me. I'm not waiting that long for you, though. The firm needs your name; I need you for a very different reason. Marry me or not, as you choose. You have three weeks. Refuse then, and I'll simply take you.'

'Threats don't frighten me!' Victoria assured him a little shakily.

'No, they excite you,' he said softly, his eyes on the frantic pulse in her throat. 'We don't have to wait that long, though. Just say the word and I'll take you home with me now.'

'The word is goodbye! I'll leave tomorrow!' She stopped dancing and he was obliged to lead her back to the table.

'I'll simply follow you,' he murmured quietly. 'The end result will be the same. If you want me to chase you I'm quite willing, but things wouldn't be settled quite as comfortably. There's this time factor, you see.'

She was shaking visibly, astonished that the other two didn't notice. Damien noticed. His eyes skimmed over her, narrowed and blue, naked desire suddenly in their intensity.

He asked Heather to dance, and she was stunned to realise that he was giving her time to recover. Against her will, her eyes followed him, drawn to the tall, superb body that moved with an animal grace. The lights caught the shining jet of his hair, the smooth power of his lean face, and she felt an almost unbearable pang of jealousy to see those long-fingered, graceful hands holding Heather Lloyd. When he bent his dark head to speak to Heather, Victoria had to turn away, aware that she couldn't bear to see his face so close to someone else, someone who was always close, in his arms.

How many women had there been in his life? How many more would there be? Some evil little demon inside her said, 'Marry him!' and her face flushed with the shock of the thoughts that had crept into her mind.

He was back before she had even begun to recover, his glance racing over her.

'I'll pick you up in the morning and take you to the works,' he offered, with a strange huskiness in his voice.

'Why?'

They were speaking as if nobody else were there, and her mind vaguely noted Heather's restless annoyance, Jeremy's tight face, but there was nothing she could do about it. Both she and Damien had discounted her decision to leave tomorrow.'

'You started a project today,' he reminded her quietly. 'I think the women would be quite pleased if you were the one to see it through to its conclusion. They seemed to take to you.'

'All right.'

They looked at each other for a long moment, until Victoria's eyes fell before the vibrant blue of his, her lashes hiding her away. For one mad moment she had been imagining what it would be like to be married to Damien, and when she looked up again he was still watching her, his eyes not cold any more.

'I—I'll be ready at eight-thirty,' she said hastily.

'No need,' he assured her quietly, his eyes locked with hers. 'They take a tea break at ten-thirty—start the meeting then and go on as long as it takes. I'll collect you at ten. Stay in bed and get some rest.'

All she could do was nod like a simpleton, and he stood, his hand helping Heather to her feet.

'Come along, Heather,' he said with a smile. 'We'll have to tear ourselves away.'

Heather would have liked to tear him away from the moment they came in, and her glance at Victoria was venomous. Damien nodded pleasantly to Jeremy, who felt the need to say the right thing, as usual.

'Why not stay with us? We'd like that, wouldn't we, Victoria?'

She didn't need to answer.

'Heather and I have other things to do,' Damien said mockingly, and the little demon in Victoria's mind changed his tune. She wanted to kill Damien at that moment, because her eyes felt hot with tears and he looked as if he knew it.

It was a look that spoke to her clearly. There was threat, possession, and satisfaction in the one glance, and she wondered if he, too, had heard the tiny demon in her mind that had earlier urged her to surrender. It was all too possible; he had always dominated her life. Apart from anything else, she was necessary to his plans. She was a Kendal.

When Damien collected her the next day, he was particularly silent. Victoria was a little nervous about the new role she had suddenly acquired, and admitted honestly that she would rather have had a few of Damien's barbed comments to gear her up than this quiet and thoughtful person, who smiled, helped her into the car, and then said nothing at all.

'How are you going to tackle this?' he enquired, as they pulled up outside the mill and entered by the big doorway under the arch.

'I'm going to talk to them, let them know about the idea and then suggest that they vote. I can't think of anything else to do.'

He nodded.

'Then what?'

'Well, assuming that they vote for Ava Hastings, she'll have to know her duties and rights. You'll be able to go over that with her later.'

'No. You will.'

'You're throwing me in at the deep end?' she asked, a trifle drily.

'I thought I was lowering you gently to your feet.' He stopped to glance down at her. 'You should have worn your executive suit,' he added, his eyes moving over her in her long, flowing skirt that just touched the top of her high boots, her fine sweater tightly belted around her slender waist. 'That shade of green always did make you look vulnerable.'

His hand cupped her head beneath the fall of silken hair, drawing her towards him, as his lips covered hers in one deep swift kiss.

'Your adrenalin needed a boost,' he said mockingly, as he released her. 'There's the tea-break bell. Go to it, princess!'

He just walked off and left her, going up to his office and never glancing back, and only then did she hear the bell—until that moment she had hazily imagined it was in her head. Bells were beginning to ring all over when Damien kissed her, just like they used to do.

There was nothing for it but to assume a businesslike look, stride into the place and see it through, but the cool air didn't last long. She was greeted like a friend, the men nodding to her, their eyes appreciative, and the women gathering round for the morning gossip, glad to have a more interesting break than usual.

When she explained things they were impressed by the speed of her actions.

'Who suggested my name?' Ava Hastings wanted to know.

'I did, as a matter of fact,' Victoria admitted, meeting the bright, intelligent eyes.

'Why me?'

'You've got a grip like steel,' Victoria assured her with a grin. 'I thought the men would think twice about scoffing at you.'

It went down very well, and they were all laughing as Joel walked in, his eyes pleased and intrigued as he waved to Victoria.

There was a whispered chorus of concern as he stopped at one of the machines.

'It's all right, Bert's headed him off.'

Victoria saw the foreman hurrying over, and turned in surprise.

'Isn't Joel allowed to touch the machines?' she asked quietly.

'Not if we can help it!'

During the burst of laughter, Ava Hastings explained to an intrigued Victoria. 'Put him near a brand new machine and he'll wreck it,' she said, with a shake of the head that showed her bewilderment. 'He understands every single process, he can talk about it for hours, that's how he sells things so well, but on the shop floor he's a menace! Mr Hunt, now,' she added with complacent admiration, 'he can do anything! I've seen him and Bert strip one of those huge machines down and put it back together again, as sweet as a daisy. He comes in and gets his jacket off, his sleeves rolled up, and he's happy as a lark. A real he-man!' she added, with a little smirk at Victoria.

'I didn't know he-men were judged on their ability to mend giant machines,' Victoria joked quickly, hoping that the colour she felt wasn't showing on her face.

'They are in these parts. I think we'll get a pin-up of him to stick in the rest-room when it's improved. The girls think he's the last word!'

Victoria was glad they were back to laughing and chattering. She was a little horrified at her own feelings. The thought of those hands that could take a machine apart, or coax her into mindless pleasure, wouldn't go out of her head. It was a rather desperate feeling, and she turned more than gladly to Joel as he came up.

'What are you doing here, Vic?' he asked in a softly indulgent voice, as the women withdrew discreetly to talk over the new turn of events that Victoria had brought about.

She told him and he was all admiration, his eyes were admiring, too.

'I've only just noticed that you're not my old playmate any more,' he said, with a very masculine glance that made her heart sink. 'I'm glad you're coming into the firm. I'll see more of you.'

'This is purely temporary,' Victoria assured him hastily. 'It's just a bit of effort for today. Damien said— we thought it was wise to show the flag for my grand-father's sake.'

'What about your own sake?' he asked softly. 'You're part of the firm.'

'Not until I'm thirty,' she said briskly. 'I'll be going back to London tomorrow.'

'Is Damien keeping to that will?' he asked angrily, a side of Joel she had never seen coming to the top.

'He has no choice,' Victoria managed hurriedly. 'I have nothing to do with the firm until then.'

'Damien can do anything, make anything happen. I'll speak to him!'

'No! Please, Joel. I don't want to be here! I——'

He took her hand and smiled down at her, looking devilishly like Damien. 'I suddenly realised that I want you to be here, Vic,' he said softly. 'You're a lot more interesting than you were when we used to make mud pies.'

She started to laugh. She just couldn't help it, and he smiled deeply into her eyes, his hand still holding hers. That was when she saw Damien.

He was just inside the doorway, his face like granite, and as the smile died on her face Joel looked up and saw him.

'Ah! Big brother! I'll just have a word with him now.'

'Oh, Joel. I wish you wouldn't.'

He gave her hair an affectionate little pull as he walked off.

'Stop worrying. He's not nearly as fierce as he looks.'

He was, he was worse. She hurried back to the women, tearing her eyes from Damien's cold, blue stare and getting straight down to business.

It took a considerable amount of nerve to go back to Damien's office later, and she wasn't quite sure whether she wanted Joel to be there or not. He wasn't, and Damien looked up impatiently as she walked in.

'Well?'

It was obviously all he was going to say, and her nerves vanished in a flood of annoyance. If he'd quarrelled with Joel, it wasn't her fault.

'All arranged. Ava Hastings is elected as the women's representative, with no opposition. It just remains for her to know exactly what she can do.'

'Anything that comes into her head, by the look of her,' he said sourly, his eyes still on the papers in front of him.

'If you distrust her, then why did you encourage this?' Victoria asked sharply, gaining herself a look as sour as his voice.

'It's necessary. You've picked out a flaw in my arrangements, and it has to be dealt with. I don't distrust Mrs Hastings any more than I distrust any other woman. She'll do as well as anyone, better than most. I'm surprised at your ability to judge character.'

'I've had a lot of practice!' Victoria snapped, tossing the notebook she carried on to the desk and preparing to walk out.

He looked up and held her gaze.

'Leaving things half-done?' he enquired scathingly. 'Joel was impressed by your dedication, impressed to the point of snarling at me. The knowledge of your ability to cut and run hasn't really penetrated his mind yet.'

'Maybe he never expected me to be more than my capabilities will allow,' she said bitterly, unbearably harassed by his constant taunting. 'He accepted me as a friend, and he's never stopped being my friend.'

'He looked a little more than friendly when I came in not long ago,' Damien murmured. 'I know you used to go about hand in hand when you were six, but it's such a long time ago. I'd better tell him that you're no longer willing to play hide and seek, except with me.'

She just looked at him bitterly, her eyes wide and accusing. He loved to fling words at her.

'Joel's my friend, my only real friend,' she said miserably, on the very edge of tears, and he got up and came round the desk, moving close, his hands on either side of her head, resting against the wall.

'It's all he can be.' His eyes were on her trembling mouth. 'You're marrying me, not my brother.'

His lips swooped to capture hers, his arms lifting her clear of the hard wall as he pressed her against him. There was no aggression in his lips. He was gentle, and, more than anything else, that gentleness released her tears. He felt the warmth of them on his face.

'Don't cry, Vicky,' he murmured. He cupped her face, his body trapping her against the wall again, his hands holding her face up to his.

'You—you've never called me that since...since...'

'Since you were a beautiful little girl, and no brat at all. You look like that now, but you're not a little girl any more. Do you know that I don't like to see you cry? I don't like to see you frightened, either, and you were frightened when I made you come into the mills.'

'I—I managed,' she whispered, stunned by his tenderness.

'If I'd thought you couldn't manage I wouldn't have left you,' he confessed softly. He looked deeply into her eyes, his own face softened. 'Marry me. Let's just stop fighting. We'll have a good marriage. We'll work at it, and you know I've always wanted you. Marry me, Vicky!' he breathed against her mouth.

There was the demon inside her, urging her on. She could hardly breathe when his lips closed over her own. Her breasts felt heavy and painful, and he drew back to look at her, his eyes sweeping over her, his hand coming to take the silken weight of her breast in his palm.

'Look at you! Why are you fighting me? Why did you ever fight me?' he asked thickly. 'You want what I want. Marry me!'

She was completely taken over by her desire, her whole world a blaze of blue eyes and possessive hands, and her arms slid around his neck, her lashes lowered to escape from the burning gaze, an almost plaintive whimper of sound on her lips.

'Victoria?' His voice was huskily soft, his body still and waiting.

'Yes.' A whisper was all she could manage, but he had no difficulty in hearing it. He collected her in his arms possessively, her slender softness moulded to him completely, a low sound deep in his throat as he claimed her mouth in a drugging kiss.

She forgot entirely where they were, those clever, capable hands made her forget, the kiss that had no end made her dazed and dizzy. All she was aware of was that she was clinging to him as she had clung to him many times before, but that this time it was different—she was a woman with a driving desire of her own now.

She heard the door open and close again, and pulled her head back to look at him in a daze.

'Heather, I should imagine,' he said huskily. 'I'd better get you back to that hotel and remember that I'm supposed to be working.' He ran his hand down the flushed silk of her cheek. 'Whatever you still have to do here had better be left until tomorrow. I think you need time to get your breath back.' His hand tightened on her face. 'No time to change your mind though!' he added, with a threat still in his voice.

She shook her head, still too bemused to move at all, and he picked up her bag, putting it into her hands and leading her out of the door, his arm possessively around her waist.

'There's a call from Japan!'

Heather's voice was sharp as she came to the door of her own office, but Damien didn't even turn.

'I'm out,' he said quietly. 'They'll ring back. Tell them an hour.'

Heather didn't answer and Victoria could tell without having seen it that it was Heather who had walked into Damien's office and seen them together. It gave her a slight twinge of fear, but even that could not penetrate the bewildered feeling that dominated her mind. The demon inside had won because she had wanted it to win. She sank into the car, still trembling, and Damien looked at her with one of those slow smiles that could tear at her heart.

He was as silent on the journey as he had been when he brought her here and, as he stopped outside the hotel, he leaned across to open the door for her. Victoria moved to get out, a little downcast that he still stayed in the car, but he took her hand and looked at her earnestly.

'I'll see you tonight,' he said quietly. 'Dinner at eight?'

She nodded, avoiding his eyes, but he showed no sign of impatience; instead, he raised her hand, his lips moving gently on the softness of her palm.

'I'll meet you downstairs,' he murmured, and she was filled with gratitude for that. If he had come up for her, she would have been utterly in his power.

CHAPTER SEVEN

IT WASN'T the easiest of afternoons. Victoria was filled with a restless energy that would not allow her to take any kind of silence. Her room seemed to be closing in on her, and she had to get out, into the open air. She drove to the house that had been her home for the whole of her life until she had run away, but, having arrived, she could not bring herself to go inside. Memories would come, memories of her grandfather, of Damien and the desperation she had felt that had forced her to London and a different life.

She left the car in the drive, and walked up the path to the top that overlooked the valley and the mills. The wind was strong up here, making her glad of the jacket she wore, and her eyes scanned the place that had been the home of her family for generations.

What would it be like married to Damien? How would he be when this desire for her had died? Would she be like those women in the family portraits: quiet, subdued, dutiful? Would Damien continue to expect her to share in the running of things, or was this small time merely a bait to trap her?

Up here it was silent, only the sound of the wind and the occasional noise of a car speeding along the valley road. She could see the spire of the church in the town— the church where she would be married, the church where Andrew Kendal was buried. The arrangement seemed so frighteningly neat. Without Damien's arms around her, her mind struggled free, and she recognised her own fear. Desire would not last, neither Damien's nor her own, and then the tight circle would close, her life moving to a well-planned pattern.

'Victoria!'

She spun round, almost frightened at the sound of a voice calling to her. She thought it was Damien who had come because he had somehow known her thoughts, her frightened doubts. It was Joel, the wind drifting his voice away and making him sound terrifyingly like this brother.

He came up the path and gained the top, the wind blowing his hair about.

'I was passing and I saw you,' he explained, his face not the smiling face she was used to. 'Did you know you could be seen so clearly from here? You're etched against the sky like those names.'

His eyes turned to the bright neon signs that seemed to dominate everything.

'Those damned names!' he gritted, his teeth clenched. 'I had one hell of a row with Damien this morning, after I left you.' He turned to her grimly. 'Why didn't you tell me the whole story when you told me about the will?' he asked angrily. 'Why didn't you tell me that Damien had you in the palm of his hand? They had no right to put you in this position. You have as much right to the mills and to your inheritance as we have!'

'It doesn't matter, Joel,' she said urgently. 'I don't want you quarrelling with Damien. Grandfather wanted the will that way and, after all, it was *his* will. When I make mine I expect I shall be determined to make it in my own way.'

'He made it in Damien's way though, didn't he?' Joel said hotly.

'Damien denies it. He says that——'

'Oh, come on, Vic!' he snapped. 'We all know how Damien is. He rules everything. I've never cared. He's better at everything than I am, and I don't resent it. We've always been close, we've been friends as well as brothers, but this thing is right back in the past, a hundred years past. It's disgusting! You get nothing until you're thirty—unless you marry him. You never told me that last little snippet of information!'

'I've told you that it doesn't matter, Joel,' she said desperately. He was so angry for her, and she had already promised to marry Damien.

'Of course it matters! He's the cleverest person I know. He could just ignore the will, or get it changed. The names can go hang for all I care. They can be torn down and nothing left up there!'

She knew that she had to tell him now. He would go on until he said something that he would always regret, and she would never have his friendship again.

'I'm going to marry Damien.' She said it with no emotion, as flatly as possible, matter-of-fact, and he stopped as if she had struck him, his eyes wide with disbelief.

'You're marrying Damien?' His voice was a shocked whisper, and she nodded blindly. 'To get your money?' He grabbed her shoulders and shook her.

'No! No! Not for that!' He didn't seem to hear; his hands were as tight and painful as Damien's.

'He was right, wasn't he?' Joel grated, his face shocked. 'I don't know you! I don't know my little playmate at all. The cold act isn't any act. It's you! You'd sell yourself to Damien for your share of the mills? What sort of a person are you, Victoria?' He turned abruptly away to go down the path, and she almost screamed after him.

'Joel! It's not true! I love him!'

He paid no attention at all, it was probably what he had expected to hear, her excuse to herself, but she heard her own voice that seemed to echo around the valley.

'I love him.'

She whispered the words again as they sank into the deep reaches of her mind. It was true. She had always loved Damien, respected and feared him and finally loved him. It had been no infatuation six years ago, it had always been there, waiting in her mind, as Damien had told her he would be. This was why he enchanted her, left her with no thought but the thought of his arms. She should have been glad, wildly happy, but she knew only a deep despair. Damien did not love her. Damien desired her, and she was the last of the Kendals anyway.

She saw Joel reach his car and slam into it, but he did not turn to either the town or the mills, he headed out towards the moors and she saw him turn to the moorland road, the car driven with blind fury until it was out of sight. She had lost Joel. She now had nobody at all.

She was quite lifeless when she went downstairs to meet Damien for dinner, and there was no way she could disguise it. She didn't have any more tricks in her repertoire. At first he was quietly annoyed, and then he became thoughtful, an even worse thing for him. They ate in almost total silence and, as the meal finished, he looked at her steadily.

'Get your coat,' he said quietly. 'We're going for a drive.'

She was obedient as a child, *more* obedient than she had been as a child, and his eyes followed her as she left the dining-room and went upstairs.

In his car there was the same brooding silence, and she only came to life as Damien stopped at her house.

'I'm not going in there!' she said urgently.

'Neither am I.'

He came and helped her out, taking her arm and turning for the moorland path.

'I don't want——!'

'Why? Is it only for you and Joel? Will it spoil the memories if I stand there with you?'

There was as much steel in his voice as in the hand that gripped her arm, and she went with him with the same lifeless expression on her face that she had shown when he arrived to dine with her.

It was cold on the top, the thin moonlight making it seem even colder, and they both stood looking down at the valley, at the red flare of names.

'I saw you this afternoon,' Damien suddenly said. 'Did you know that from my office window I can see this place? If I get up and walk to the window and look out towards the moors, I can see these heights. I can see Victoria's throne. This afternoon I could see Victoria— when she came up here to meet my brother.'

'I didn't.'

She made no effort to deny it hotly. It was just the truth. She had come up here to escape from her room at the hotel, to escape from the growing fear of what she had agreed to.

'He was here!'

'I never said he wasn't. He saw me too.'

'He was holding you!'

She turned away, her eyes misting over with tears.

'No, not like that. He was angry. He said he had quarrelled with you and he was angry with me for not telling him about the will. I—I told him some of it before, but not the part about—about——'

'About the need to marry me,' he finished for her. 'It's not the first time that Joel and I have had a quarrel; he does have a smattering of my temper. He blamed you for not giving him the sordid details?'

'You gave him those,' Victoria accused quietly. 'He had no need to know.'

'I didn't give him any more details than he already had. He went to see Gresham after our initial spat. He was determined to see if the will could be broken, his fondness for you demanding fair play. Gresham is not as young as he was, and I doubt if he ever had much sense. He just blurted the whole thing out to Joel. *Then* we had what might reasonably be called a quarrel—a real one, no holds barred. I had to order him out.'

He was standing with his back to her, his hands in his pockets, his eyes on the red flare in the sky. It suddenly came to her that he looked lonely.

'I'm sorry. I assumed that——'

'Yes, you always assume, don't you?' he said, almost wearily. 'I should be used to it by now. Why are you marrying me, Victoria?' he asked quietly.

'Because you want me to, and——'

'Victoria!' He spun round and grasped her face, tilting it to the moonlight. 'Why!' he asked violently. 'For pity's sake, be honest for once! Tell me you want me!'

She was shocked into silence and he let her go, half turning away.

'All right. I know it's for the money.'

'It's not!' she cried bitterly. 'Whatever Joel thinks, it's not that. I told you what I was going to do. I don't need the money, now or ever! I can go back now and sign a contract for a year in America, and the pay is——'

'No!'

He pulled her into his arms, looking down into her pale face before his head dropped and his face was hidden in her hair. 'I want to see you every day, every night, wake up with my arms around you, your head on my pillow. If I tell you . . .' He stopped and looked up at her with eyes so blazing that they glittered even in the dim light. 'Leave me and I'll follow you till hell freezes over!' he ended harshly.

They looked at each other almost warily, but she saw a sort of desperation in his eyes, and she reached up wonderingly to touch his face. Her thoughts were frozen on to the one thought that she loved him.

He gathered her close, his lips seeking hers almost sweetly.

'Vicky,' he murmured in a deep voice like the darkness around. 'Sometimes you look so much as you used to look. Sometimes I forget the years. I'll not be happy until I hear you say the words, until we stand at the altar.' He looked down at her in the darkness, the lights on her face. 'Once, you told me that you loved me, and I believed you. I don't need any words like that now. I don't care why you're marrying me. I only care that you are.'

She looked at him forlornly. She remembered too. She remembered he had not ever said those words to her. But how could he? It was all for the mills, all for Kendal and Hunt. Tears swam in her eyes, and in spite of the darkness, he saw them.

'Vicky, Vicky!' he said softly. 'I promise you no cause to cry.' He rocked her close, but the tears still fell. How could he promise that? There would be no love at all.

Victoria was still bemused the next day. His eyes were smiling at her as she came down to meet him and be driven to the works to finish her task with the women.

It was easy, and she was thankful for that. She felt so dazed herself that any trouble would have knocked her over, but they were solidly behind her and she took the good-natured ragging of the men in her stride, happy to finalise all the arrangements and go up to Damien's office before lunch.

He wasn't in, but she sat down to wait, her heart drumming like mad at the thought that he would suddenly walk through the door. Her feelings for him were getting out of control.

It was Heather Lloyd who walked through the door, her face strangely triumphant as she stopped and looked across at Victoria.

'Well, I wondered why you were hanging around here,' she said with a look that contained scorn. 'I expect you're busy trying to work your way into Damien's heart?'

'Damien and I are going to be married in two weeks!' Victoria snapped, deciding to wipe the smile off Heather's face right away.

It didn't. The scorn simply grew.

'It's no surprise to me. If you were expecting to shock me, then forget it. Funny, though, I always thought you were a kind of deep-rooted goody. I never imagined you'd be willing to marry somebody for money.'

'What are you talking about?'

Victoria jumped up, but Heather simply walked to Damien's desk and put the late mail there.

'I know all about the will,' she said scathingly. 'Marry him, do! He'll get what he wants—everything! You'll get your money, but I'll have Damien. You needn't look shocked. I've been after him for years, but finally it was Damien who came after me. Working here was his idea. Why do you think that was? We'll go on just as before, weekends away, nights at the office, nights at my place when nobody's there. It's a comfortable arrangement. I've always known he had to marry you.'

She walked out and Damien came in almost immediately, the smile dying on his face when he saw her.

'What's the matter?' He walked to her and took her shoulders in his hands. 'Victoria?'

'How could you!' She pulled away and turned from him. 'How could you tell anyone about the will? Especially her!'

'What are you talking about? I never told anyone, not even Joel. You imagine I would tell Heather?'

'She knows! How else could she know? When did you tell her? After you left me last night?'

He went white to the lips, his hands hard as he jerked her against him.

'After I left you last night, I went home! I was frustrated, but I was alone!' His face suddenly became thoughtful. 'She heard Joel yelling at me. She must have come back in while he was here yesterday.'

'Oh, *please*!' she said scornfully. 'I've just had the news from Heather. She's always known you had to marry me. Always is a long time, Damien!'

'So my words won't do?' he grated.

'It doesn't matter,' Victoria said dully. 'It was always ridiculous, and you know that as well as I do. Now it's impossible.'

'What do you mean?' There was so much menace in his voice that she had to use all her courage to stand up to him.

'You know deep down why I'm marrying you,' she managed coolly, her heart threatening to break at the look in his eyes. 'The whole valley suspects that I came back for the money, the "loot" as you so rightly said. Do you imagine Heather Lloyd will keep quiet? If I marry you they'll know they were right. I don't think I could live with that, even for the money. I'm not even going to try.'

'If you think you're going to take off a second time——' he began, and she was relieved almost to the point of tears as Bert the foreman knocked briefly and stuck his head in the door.

'Number one is going on the blink!' he said urgently.

Damien didn't even turn. He just swore bitterly and kept on gripping Victoria's shoulders. Bert was not at all put out, though. He had worked with Damien's father, taught Damien most of what he knew.

'There's a roll half-way through. We'll lose the whole damned lot, Damien!' He let her go, but with so much reluctance that she knew he was considering leaving the machine to do as it wished, grind to a halt or chew up an expensive roll of cloth. It was only the need to get rid of Bert that made him even think of moving.

'I'm coming!' He snapped out the words at Bert, who left muttering to himself.

'Stay here!' he said menacingly. 'Stay here until I come back. I intend to get to the bottom of this once and for all!'

She nodded numbly, but her mind was working quickly and, as she heard him go down the steps, she moved fast. He had collected her this morning, and he would imagine she was stranded here, but she was relying on his trust in this place. In London she was used to locking her car securely, taking the keys away. At the works, Damien never did that, she had noticed. She prayed he had not done that now.

She ran down to the Ferrari and saw the keys in the ignition. If she crashed it she would face things then, but right now she was too desperate to care. She heard the low growl of the powerful engine and swung the car away in a tight turn, racing up the drive to the road and making for her hotel.

'Get my bill ready now!' She just snapped out the order as she made for the stairs and her room, and she was throwing things into her suitcases in seconds. By the time she came down, struggling with her own cases rather than wait for help, her bill was ready, and she was signing the cheque as the telephone rang.

'Why, yes! She's here right now, Mr Hunt.' The receptionist looked at Victoria questioningly, half holding the phone out to her.

'Tell him I'm going back down to the works this minute,' Victoria said as calmly as she could. 'I'll be there almost at once.'

It seemed to work, and she was shakily relieved that she had been right there. If she had not been available, the man would have probably told Damien she was checking out. She took his keys from her bag.

'In case I miss him, can you give him these?' she murmured in an off-hand voice.

'Certainly, Miss Kendal.'

It was all so easy. She just needed to keep her nerve. The car she had been using since she had come home was also outside. It was her grandfather's car, immaculate but old, and she stepped into it and left at once. Half-way along the road to the motorway, though, she realised just how foolish she was. She had an image in her mind of the sleek, red Ferrari, Damien at the wheel, as he came chasing her to demand explanations, to subdue and enslave her again. He would catch her. By now he would have rung the hotel again and this time he would get the whole story. He would get a lift there and collect his car, and he would catch her long before she even reached the motorway.

She turned into a side road, cutting across country and making for the nearest station, praying she had out-thought him, her eyes constantly in the rear-view mirror, expecting to see the red car screaming up behind her.

She left the car at the station, leaving the keys in an envelope, and leaving, too, a five pound note with one of the porters to deliver the envelope to Joel, his name and address clearly written on the front. Then she caught a train to Leeds, where she changed for York and the main line to London. But, even as the train left York Station, she was nervously alert, expecting to see his tall, furious form striding on to the platform. Only when they were well out and the fast train was heading for London could she relax—even then she dared not think. Thinking was too painful altogether. She suddenly felt adrift. The thought of Damien's arms made her choke with grief.

Once in London she went straight to her flat, but she knew she could not stay there. Damien had come here with her when he had originally come to collect her when her grandfather had died. She could not even be sure that he would leave things until morning. She packed another suitcase and left, making for a hotel as far away as possible. She had enough money to live like this for the time being and, even if it took the few thousand her grandfather had left her, she dared not face Damien. Only when she was safely locked in the small, drab bedroom could she breathe easily. He would not find her now. She was safe.

Three days later, it all seemed to have worked. Such was the power of Damien that she had at first been uneasy about venturing out of her hotel, but there was her living to earn and, in any case, even if he came there was little he could do here in a city. She asked herself just what she was expecting him to do. She feared herself more than she feared Damien. Being safe meant not being anywhere at all near to him—staying out of his arms. If he looked at her, held her, she was likely to promise anything. She told herself that he would not come. After all, when she had originally left home he had come only once. Even so, his voice seemed to ring in her ears, 'Leave me and I'll follow you till hell freezes over!'

She only contacted her agent by telephone. She was already well-known and it would be quite easy for Damien to discover who her agent was. He had been to the showing at Madame Gautier's salon, and that woman would tell a man like Damien anything. He knew nothing else, though, and she had a backlog of work to do, especially for Dale West. She felt safe with Dale.

He was delighted to see her, and they had so much gossip to catch up on that working with him was quite exhausting.

'You'll be too rich to work now, Victoria,' he said, as he arranged lights and background to the shot. 'Does it mean I'll have to look for somebody else?'

'Not likely! I don't get anything worth speaking of until I'm thirty.'

'Thirty!' He darted out from behind his equipment to look at her in astonishment. 'I say, that's a bit stiff! Still, your grandfather was a little on the old-fashioned side, wasn't he? Now, I got my legacy straight off with no fuss or bother, even though it's not a great big textile firm.'

'You've got a legacy? How marvellous! Tell me about it.'

'A little to the left, darling. Yes, that's it. No movement in these shots.' He fussed endlessly, she thought in amusement, but his shots were fabulous and she usually obeyed.

'I hope it's not going to take long, Dale. It's quite chilly in here this morning, and I'm not exactly dressed for the conditions,' she murmured wryly. She was in a diaphanous creation of silk organza with a low neckline studded with rhinestones, the briefest undies beneath, a provocative and sensuous garment, but Dale eyed her coolly, his mind merely on the shot.

'Sorry,' he muttered briefly. 'I have to think about the optimum temperature for this type of film.'

'Whereas I'm quite expendable,' Victoria continued for him, with an amused look at his intense preparations. 'Keep my mind occupied. What about your legacy?'

'A great-aunt, darling! I've been left an island.'

'How wonderful!' She moved, and was instantly chastised.

'My great-uncle was a bit of an oddity, actually,' he told her, as he moved round his equipment, still fussing. 'He bought this land that nobody wanted and moved there lock, stock and barrel, dragging Auntie with him. It's an island in a river, believe it or not, in North Wales. I went there when I was a boy, and was quite fascinated. There was this keep thing on top of the hill, and he had it pulled down and turned into a house. You can only reach the place by a long bridge. He had the bridge built with total disregard for anyone else. It was in the days before planning permission, of course, and he owned the stretch of river. It infuriated fishermen, ramblers and the like. He wasn't a popular man, I can tell you.'

He came round and moved her position again, and then adjusted the lights.

'I'll take you down there to see it one day, when we're not too busy,' he offered absently. 'All set now. We'll begin.'

Talking was definitely over. Dale was the most pleasant and helpful of men, but in the studio he was a tyrant. Victoria went into a cool dream, knowing exactly which expression he was wanting, the praise and encouragement he muttered under his breath telling her she was right.

'For heaven's sake!'

Dale snapped out the words as a draught of air told him that someone had entered the studio, and he spun round. Victoria held her pose, trying to keep the expression on her face. Whoever had simply walked in was about to find out that Dale West was not as easygoing in here as he was outside.

'What do you want? I'm working!' Dale glared with narrowed eyes through the lights, almost as blinded as Victoria would have been had she turned her head.

'It's not what I want, it's *who* I want! I want *her*! The work can stop right now, if that's what it's called.'

Damien's voice, darkly angry, froze Victoria on the spot, and he strode further in, moving Dale aside as if he were a puny object, his eyes blazing as he stared down at Victoria.

'Do I take you dressed, or like that?' he asked violently, ignoring Dale. 'Now that you've added car theft to your list of indiscretions, I don't expect that going out looking like the Queen of Sheba would bother you too much!'

'I left your car! I even left grandfather's car keys, although that was nothing to do with you.'

'We're in the middle of shooting!' Dale protested loudly and uselessly.

'And what happens after that?' Damien grated through clenched white teeth, slanting him a violent look. 'I'll give you thirty seconds,' he told Victoria. 'Models can dress and undress quickly, I believe. I know *you* can!'

'This is costing me money!' Dale informed him irritably.

'It would have cost you a lot more than money if you hadn't been behind that camera when I walked in!' Damien said, with such menace that Dale stepped back quickly. 'I'll wait in the office,' he said to Victoria, ignoring Dale completely. 'I'll extend your time to two minutes, as you've got so much to put on.'

If she hadn't been white with rage, she would have been red with embarrassment, and she got up quickly, her hands clenched tightly by her sides.

'I'm going nowhere at all!' she snapped furiously. 'Who do you think you are?'

'You know who I am!' he rasped, his eyes running over her, angry and probing, making her realise that the lighting was doing exactly what it was meant to do from this angle. 'Two minutes,' he added softly, 'then I come back in and you'll really know it.'

He strode out and slammed the door and Victoria moved faster than she had moved in her life.

'He's mad,' Dale said in a whisper.

'I believe you! I'm leaving by the back door. He may kill you, Dale, but it's all in a good cause—my cause!'

She rushed into the changing-room, the door partly open, and Dale stood outside whispering urgently.

'He'll come to your flat. When he came for you before he went with you there.'

'I'm in a hotel. I'll go back there and think this out. I don't know where to go after that.'

'Give me the name of your hotel and I'll come round later, I've got the glimmerings!' Dale said urgently.

'No way! He'll shake you like a wet mop until you tell him.'

'He won't. How do I know where you live? I'll show him your card with that address. That's all I know.'

'All right.' She darted out, her eyes fearfully on the door to the office, whispered the name of her hotel and then left by the back door, a door artistically screened by curtains, invisible to the casual observer. When Damien came in he would take Dale apart.

She signalled frantically for a taxi, and sank thankfully inside. She was a coward! Every time Damien was near she was prepared to run, and she knew perfectly well why. She dared not be trapped in a loveless marriage. She loved him too much. It would destroy her utterly. Her battle with Damien was a fight for survival, as it had always been. Close to him she went down in the tide of his passion, willing to drown. It was only when she was away from him that she could look at things at all clearly. He still wanted what her grandfather had wanted, and his desire for her was merely a bonus—a bonus for him.

Dale came later that evening looking like a conspirator, so very obvious that she was sure Damien would have followed him.

'What did he say?' she asked rather fearfully.

'Nothing.' Dale looked at her seriously. 'He said nothing at all. It was the most worrying thing he could have done. I was all geared up to put up a great show of resistance, and it wasn't necessary. He came in almost as you left and looked round slowly. I told him you'd gone the back way and he just looked at me, so I hastily showed him your card. He's more worrying when he's silent than when he's raging.'

Victoria nodded a little anxiously. She knew that.

'What am I going to do?'

She sat with her hands clenched between her knees. One part of her wanted to run, another part of her wanted to go back and wait at home for Damien, accepting things on any basis just to be with him.

'I can't sit here each day and hide.'

'You don't want to go back to him?' Dale asked astutely.

She had explained nothing, but he knew her fairly well, and there had been no mistaking the angry possession about Damien. He had not come for her like a brother.

'I can't.'

'Well, then,' he said smugly, 'how would you like to borrow an island?'

CHAPTER EIGHT

THE DESCRIPTION was a little overstated, Victoria thought as she stopped her car and looked at Dale's 'island'. It was the most peculiar place she had ever seen, and she could well believe that his great-uncle had been a peculiar man. It had taken hours to reach, as it was deep in the wilderness of North Wales. He had warned her to come well-stocked with provisions, and she was thankful she had done that, because there had not been any sign of humanity for the last ten miles or more, and then only isolated cottages that may well have merely been holiday homes.

Now, at the other side of the bridge that had brought Dale's great-uncle enemies and notoriety, she sat in her car and looked at her latest hideaway. It was more of a lump in the river than an island, she mused wryly. It rose above the water with an irritation all its own. Perhaps if the old keep that Dale had mentioned had been left there, and the place left untouched, it would not have looked quite so incongruous, but a substantial cottage had been built right in the middle of it with no thought for artistic positioning, but merely for geometrical exactitude. His great-uncle had wanted it in the centre, and that was exactly where it was. The thought of mod cons uneasily entered her mind, but she shrugged them away. Beggars could not be choosers, and she was, after all, on the run like any common criminal.

She took one last, hopeless look, and then started the car again. The bridge looked substantial, being made from the same stone as the cottage. Had Dale's great-uncle used the stone of the old keep to make this bridge too? It must have been some keep!

She wondered if it had been an old mine-shaft, but thoughts like that didn't help, they only made her scared, and when she was scared she always thought about Damien and the strength of his arms. Dale's great-uncle wasn't the only one who was peculiar!

The car went over the bridge with no sign of impending disaster. The bridge was well-built and strong, just wide enough for one car, and she drove as close to the cottage as she could before getting out and looking around. The river was deep and swift-running, sounding pleasant and soothing in the mid-day sun, but the small island was barren and drab, a few stunted bushes clothing the slopes that led to the house, an unkempt garden that looked as if it had been abandoned for centuries surrounding the front door. She got out the key, which was big enough to have been the original key to the keep, and opened the door with some misgivings.

They were well justified. It looked damp, it smelled damp, and she almost backed straight out. It was so far from civilisation, though, and she had been driving for hours. It would have to do. She looked around with wry amusement. Dale was so fastidious—obviously he had not been here since he was an impressionable boy. If he came now he would shudder. Luckily she had brought bedding—he had warned her of that, and a dangerous expedition to her flat had been well worthwhile. Damien had probably gone back in disgust. He couldn't spend all his time looking for her—he had several businesses to run.

She thrust the thought of him out of her mind, and began to settle in. Maybe she would grow to love the place. It seemed unlikely. She began to open windows to let the warm air into the damp atmosphere, and then she went upstairs, dragging the mattress from the bed and letting it fall by itself to the bottom of the stairs before struggling outside with it. She heaved it up on top of the car and left it in the sun.

It took the rest of the day to get some sort of order and comfort and, as the light began to fade, she brought wood inside from the old shed at the back to make a fire, propping the mattress at one side of it as she sat at the other and ate the first meal she had made since she arrived.

There was no electricity, but there must have been a hundred candles in a wooden box in the small kitchen, and the two oil-lamps were quite full. She had learned several new skills since she arrived, and the mod cons were there—in a way. The water came from a huge tank behind the cottage that made the place look more ugly than ever, but by some ingenious route it reached the old taps and flushed the elaborate hand-painted loo. She would have to be very sparing. Obviously the tank was there to catch rain-water—good for her hair, but definitely a finite commodity.

She found herself going off to sleep in the old but surprisingly comfortable chair, and she roused herself sufficiently to take the mattress up the stairs with more cunning than strength, and make the bed in the small room that looked down on to the racing river. It was a good place for a Boy Scout camp, she thought ruefully as she fell asleep—by the end of the week she would look like a gypsy, and every nail would be broken.

Victoria slept deeply though, not awakening until the sun touched her face and the warmth made her stir. Her heart gave a small leap of shock until she remembered exactly where she was, and then she got out of bed and stood looking down at the river. This morning it looked friendly, and she felt a great burst of high spirits. She was miles away from everyone, with nothing to fear, nobody to please.

She felt the surge of energy she used to have when she was fifteen. She dressed in jeans and a shirt, washed hastily, and made the sort of breakfast she hadn't eaten for years. She took it outside and sat on the step, eating hungrily as she watched the sunlight on the river. She was as secure as if this were a fortress, and not a soul knew where she was but Dale.

Victoria had a peaceful day. A thorough search of the cottage showed her where everything was, and the only thing that would pose any problem was that with there being no electricity, there was no fridge. She stood the milk in the river at a place close by where the swirling water was icily cold, and after a further search she found two plastic containers, which she washed thoroughly and then placed the meat she had brought inside. That too was submerged in the river, strings securing it to the bank, and she retreated to the cottage for lunch with a wide grin on her face. At this rate she would be able to take over a Scout Patrol herself.

As evening drew on, though, her rather smug elation began to drain away. The night before she had been too busy and too tired to suffer from any nerves. Now, as the night steadily advanced, she began to feel very isolated. She told herself that isolation was exactly what she had wanted, but uneasy thoughts began to creep into her mind. How did she know that the whole area was deserted? She had followed a road to this place—someone else could do the same thing. The lights from the house would be visible for a long way in the scarcely populated landscape. What would she do if anyone crossed the bridge, knocked on the door? She could hardly pretend that she was not in. She would though!

She made her evening meal and sat by the fire as darkness became complete, and even the racing river took on a menacing sound. She shook her fears away, telling herself that this was merely a result of the strain she had been under since her grandfather's death, and not some premonition of disaster.

Even so, when she had washed the dishes and put them away, she went carefully round the cottage checking that the windows were tightly secure, and that both the back and the front doors were locked. She drew the curtains even more tightly together, and went up to bed with the certain knowledge that she was not going to sleep a wink.

It was about midnight when a noise woke her, and she tried to remember what it was—whether it was the tail-end of a dream or some real noise. It was silent now, though, and she began to drift off to sleep again, only to shoot up in bed wide-eyed with fear as someone knocked heavily on the front door.

Her decision to pretend she was not there became somewhat weakened as she thought of several possibilities. Suppose they thought the house was empty? Suppose they then broke a window to get in? She slid out of bed and peered through the curtains, chewing her lips with vexation as she found that it was impossible to see anything. There was total blackness outside—she couldn't even make out the outline of her own car.

Whoever was there was now hammering again, trying the handle, and she ran silently downstairs to listen behind the front door. There was only the dying glow of the fire, and she dared not light one of the candles. She groped around for her handbag, her hand checking that her car keys were there, and then she quickly un-locked the back door, before going back to silently unlock the front door too. The next time they tried the handle the door would open. She flew to the back door and stepped outside, her heart hammering violently, her ear to the crack she had left open. When the intruder stepped inside she would race round to the front and get into her car.

She heard the front door open and she began to run, stumbling on the uneven, stony ground, her breath small gasps in her throat as she rushed with little caution round to the front. Even then she could not see the car, and as she did spot it she was grasped firmly by two hands that seemed to come at her out of the night.

The scream that rose in her throat failed to materialise, and wild thoughts raced through her mind. How many times had she thought when reading of someone being attacked, 'Why didn't they scream?' She couldn't—her fear was too great. It paralysed her!

Small sounds of panic were all that would come from her tight throat, and she hardly heard the voice until her name was spoken in a loud, uncompromising command.

'Victoria! Be still, Victoria.'

'Damien!' She gasped his name in disbelief, her arms winding tightly around his neck as he lifted her into his arms and shouldered the cottage door open wide.

'Where the hell are the lights?'

He stood her down for a second, and she heard the click of his lighter as he flicked it into flame and glanced angrily around. He pounced on the candle that stood by the door on an old oak table, and then he pounced on her.

'What the devil are you doing racing around outside in the pitch black? You could have fallen headlong into that river!'

His eyes blazed at her in the candle-light, and then he saw the state she was in. She was leaning against the door where he had placed her; her feet muddy and scraped by the hard stones, her nightie splattered with mud at the hemline, and her body trembling from head to foot.

'Hell! You're quite mad. I don't know how you survive at all.'

He lifted her and carried her to the chair by the dying fire, removing his jacket and placing it around her where she could snuggle shivering against the warmth, and then he lit every candle he could see and added wood to the fire.

'Explain to me this insanity,' he said quietly, still crouched close by, his eyes on the growing flames.

'I didn't—I didn't know who it was. I——'

'Didn't you hear my car? Didn't you hear me shouting to you as I first came to the door?'

'I—I was asleep. I stayed awake a long time, but then I fell asleep and I must have been too——'

He didn't let her finish. He turned to her impatiently, still crouched by her.

'You had no idea it was me?'

'No! If I *had* known I wouldn't have run out. I thought it was someone trying to get in.'

'So you decided to help them?' he asked in an astonished voice.

'I thought if I let them get in by the front door as I left by the back, I could get to my car and drive away.'

'Andrew always had his head screwed on the right way,' he mused scathingly. 'I'm beginning to wonder about you!'

His eyes glanced down at her feet and he drew in a seething breath through his teeth.

'Does this place have a kitchen?'

At her anxious nod he got up and went out of the room, coming back with a bowl of water and a towel. She had not moved at all. Movement was quite beyond her, and she sat in a dazed manner as he bathed her feet and dried them thoroughly.

'How did you find me?'

She was very quiet and he glanced up at her sharply.

'I asked West.'

'Dale would never have told you.'

Damien's sceptical look assured her that she was an unworldly fool.

'His devotion to you does not override his commercial interests,' he said scathingly, standing and moving the bowl aside.

'You bribed him? I don't believe it!'

'No, I didn't bribe him. I planted myself in his studio and threatened to stay there until he disclosed your whereabouts. The models refused to work in front of an audience.' He smiled tightly. 'It's not easy to pose in the nude when a sceptical visitor sits there looking.'

'Dale doesn't do nude photography!' Victoria said sharply, her face flushed.

'Oh, I admit that *he* was dressed,' Damien taunted. 'In any case, he gets pretty close to it from what I saw of you.'

She sprang up and glared at him.

'I was not nude! The shots would have come out quite beautifully. The lights would cover almost——'

'The lights were a great help. I didn't need long to get a close inspection.'

'You had no right to be there!'

'And West had?' he asked, with a soft-voiced violence that started her shivering all over again.

'Oh, for pity's sake!' he muttered. 'Go back to bed.'

'I have to lock the doors. I have to——'

'I'm here! I'll lock the doors if you still feel worried.' He looked at her impatiently. 'Do those feet hurt?'

'No. Thank you for——'

'I imagine I caused it in the first place,' he growled.

'Do you want a meal?' she asked anxiously, wondering why she wasn't ordering him out—not that he would have gone. She was horrified to discover how much she wanted him here.

'I ate on the way down. After West described this place, I thought I'd better stock up on food. No electricity? What do you do for a fridge?'

'I put the meat and milk in the river and I tied it with strings.'

'Heaven help us!' he muttered derisively. 'Go to bed before I collapse with shock. A practical butterfly. I'll have to sleep on that one!'

'Where do you imagine you're going to sleep?' she asked unwisely, her temper beginning to grow over her delight at being able to look at him.

He gave a wolfish smile that had her cheeks flushing, but his eyes turned to the side of the room.

'I would think on that couch, settee, sofa, or whatever it is.'

'I think it's a bed-settee,' Victoria said huffily.

'It may imagine that, too,' he remarked. 'Time will tell, however.'

'I've got no blankets for you,' she informed him. 'You're going to be cold.

'Don't sound so gleeful—I've brought bedding,' he countered. 'When West tells something, he tells all. I'm prepared for anything.'

'Pity I'm not!' Victoria snapped making for the stairs!'

'We'll see,' he murmured softly, his voice as deep as the night. 'For now, though, you look in need of some sleep after all that excitement, and I'm tired from driving and struggling with you.'

She just turned round and went upstairs, and he ignored her totally. In bed, she heard him go out to his car, which seemed to be a long way from the cottage, and then he locked the doors. He was still wandering about when she went to sleep, and her mind fought against the fact that she felt safe, secure—almost happy in spite of her temper.

* * *

In the morning he was up and in the kitchen when she came downstairs. There was no sign of anger, and that in itself was worrying, after the trouble she had caused. He was cooking breakfast, and he didn't even glance up at her.

'Ready in two minutes,' he said crisply. 'We'll need a hearty breakfast.'

'Before we leave, you mean?' she asked rebelliously. 'You're going, but I'm not!' She couldn't take her eyes away from those strong, capable hands, and when she looked up he was watching her stealthy fascination.

'I was thinking of the fresh air. It gives one an appetite.' He looked away and carried on with his self-appointed task. 'We're not leaving,' he added softly.

'If you refuse to go, then I'm leaving,' Victoria managed quickly, her heart beginning to thunder at his tone.

'Tell me how?' He didn't stop and as she stared at him wildly he put her breakfast on the table and sat down to his.

She marched to the door, determined to pack her car and leave at once, but the sight that met her eyes stopped all such thoughts. No wonder his car had seemed to be so far away last night! It was parked at the bridge, totally blocking any exit. There was no way of even sliding past it with a bicycle. He had her securely trapped unless she left on foot.

She turned on him furiously, but he ignored her and simply went on eating.

'I can wait you out,' she said bitterly. 'I don't have several business to run.'

He didn't answer, and that was terribly upsetting. There was nothing to do but sit down and eat, the silence almost painful.

'How did you know about Dale?' she asked at last, unable to bear the quiet any more.

'The sexy Madame Gautier directed me to your agent, who led me to West. Easy, my pet. One step at a time.'

'I won't go back,' she muttered unhappily. 'I don't want to go back, and I don't want to marry you. The valley will just have to take care of itself. If necessary, I'll have it sitting on my conscience.'

He nodded with no appearance of concern.

'I understand. It doesn't matter. We'll stay here for a while and then go to some other place.'

'What do you mean?'

Victoria sprang up and stood looking down at him as he raised his handsome head, his face quite calm.

'You've just told me you never want to go back,' he reminded her. 'You're concerned about what people will say; you won't marry me. All I'm saying is that I understand. Don't marry me. We'll stay here and then go to some other place. Married or not, I want you. I told once that I'd thought of kidnapping you——'

'I was here first!' she gasped. 'I—I mean you can't just——'

'I agree that it's an unusual way of conducting a kidnapping,' he said thoughtfully, 'but it's as good a way as any, actually. Saves a lot of messy struggling. Better than putting a bag over your head, don't you think?'

She stared at him wildly.

'Are you joking? You've always looked quite sane. It never occurred to me that you had a loose slate!'

He continued to look up at her, his blue eyes dancing.

'I want you, my precious. I've come for you. What's so mad about that?'

'I never meant that I'd—I'd live with you!'

His eyes skimmed over her, his gaze narrow and brilliantly blue, the laughter dying. 'Then you just hadn't thought it through to the end, had you?' he asked softly.

'If you imagine that I——'

'I don't need imagination,' he said quietly. 'I know.'

His eyes locked with hers, and her face flushed painfully. He knew exactly how she felt when he touched her. He had always known. All she had done recently was prove it. She turned and walked out of the house but there was no way of escaping. She sat by the river angrily tossing pebbles into it, and after a while he joined her, standing to look down at her steadily, saying nothing.

'If you think you can just come to me and demand——' she began heatedly, but he stopped her before she could finish.

'I won't come to you and demand anything. You'll come to me and beg. Desire is a two-edged sword and I'm quite accustomed to waiting. I've waited a long time, even when you were there. Now *I'm here*. There's nobody for miles, no let-up, no escape! You'll come to me, Victoria, and we both know it.'

It was an uneasy morning. Victoria had no place now to escape from the tension that Damien was building slowly and deliberately. If she simply walked away, he would follow, and there was little she could do about that. In any case, they were miles from anywhere, and the danger lay not with Damien but with herself. All she had to do was keep out of his way—no easy thing in the confined space of the island.

She went indoors initially and he wandered around, looking with rueful amusement at the facilities of the river island. Victoria washed the breakfast dishes, made her bed, and was then left with nothing at all to do. When Damien came inside, she promptly went out and returned to her desultory occupation of tossing pebbles into the river.

There had to be some way of getting the better of him, and her chance came when she saw him walk around to the wood-shed and bring wood into the cottage. He was making a fire, and she stalked across to the open doorway, looking in at him.

'If you're going to make a fire so early you'll have to get more logs ready,' she said acrimoniously. 'There's plenty of wood in that shed, but most of it is too big to burn on this fire. If you burn it now we'll be without a fire later, and I don't know why you want a fire now anyway!'

He was crouched before the old grate, looking up at her with an exaggerated expression of astonishment.'

'Your practical ways astound me,' he said ironically. 'I'll do it now, then, while the day is young. I have to have a fire though. You see, it's so cool and unfriendly here.'

It made her feel ridiculous. Damien never had much trouble in making her blush and feel like a fool. She felt more angry than ever now, and looked at him with sparkling green eyes.

'What did you expect? You left your friend behind. I expect it's hot enough whenever she's there!'

He stood slowly and sauntered over to her, his hand resting on the door-frame as he looked down at her.

'Do I detect malice? Your envy is showing.'

He was so tall and dark, she thought wonderingly. His voice was almost sleepily indulgent. It was difficult to even take her eyes from him, impossible to move away. A great flare of awareness surged over her. She was here, miles from anywhere, alone with Damien.

'Vicky?'

His arm curled round her waist, moving her forward, and she came without a struggle, her eyes locked with his.

'Don't call me that,' she said in a softly fretful voice.

'Right now, you look like that.' His eyes scanned her face. 'At this moment, I know only too well why I want to marry you.'

He stood upright and brought her closer, his free hand stroking her hair, and when she simply went on looking at him he suddenly caught her tightly to him, his mouth covering hers, opening to meet her submission as her lips parted.

It was what she wanted, she admitted to herself, her mind and body dazzled by her feelings for Damien. Every part of her yearned to belong to him, and she felt a wave of pleasure that was almost wicked as he brought her fiercely against his hard body.

To know that he still wanted her made her feel more feminine than she had ever felt, and her arms wound around his neck as she moulded herself into him willingly.

His hands stroked her back and moved down to her thighs, tension and danger in his fingertips, and she suddenly had a vivid picture of him like this with someone else. Heather! Jealousy burned through her, and she tore her lips away, pulling free of his arms, leaving him looking at her with almost dazed eyes.

'You little bitch!' It was a contemptuous whisper, the heated look dying from his face, leaving him pale and angry. He grasped her slender shoulders, his fingers biting into her flesh. 'Try that again and I'll take you with no hesitation whatsoever. I'll forget that you were a little girl once. I'll just remember what you turned into!'

He pushed her aside and strode angrily around the corner of the cottage, bending to scoop up the old axe as he passed, and she stood still for only one second. She had to get away. Every time he touched her she would yield, and it was all merely a matter of time.

Her bag was on the table and she snatched it up—there was no time to take anything but that. This time, though, she did not race out. The memory of those strong hands grasping her as he had arrived was still very fresh in her mind, and her progress to the Ferrari was quiet and stealthy.

She had taken his car before, and it would be easy to do it again. This time he would be utterly stranded. She looked quickly into her bag and made sure that her own car keys were there. She didn't intend to leave him any way of getting out of here, unless he could somehow start her car without keys. Even if he could, he would never catch the Ferrari once she was away—he wasn't the only one who could drive.

It stood there on the cottage side of the bridge, and her spirits plunged a little as she realised she would have to back out over the bridge if she was to escape. She would have to do it fast, too. Once that engine started to growl he would hear it, and there was no sound of wood being chopped—he was probably still too furious to begin.

When she reached the car she felt that her goal had already been achieved, and she eased herself quietly into the driving seat. She would have to leave her clothes and everything else behind, but it didn't matter at all—all that mattered was escape, to get far away. She closed the door quietly and reached for the keys.

They weren't there! She had been sure they would be. Her mind had seen them there as they had been before, and she looked at the dashboard in complete disbelief. Where would he have put them? She began to search frantically, knowing perfectly well that time was running out, but they were neither under the mat nor anywhere else.

She looked up in frustration, her heart leaping with painful fright as she saw Damien standing in front of the car, the keys dangling from his tantalising fingers, his eyes filled with angry derision, and there was nothing left to do but get out and admit defeat.

'You once said you didn't step into the same hole twice,' he reminded her caustically. 'You imagine I do? I have a very vivid memory of the last time you took my car.'

'You knew what I was going to do, and you just let me!' she accused bitterly.

'I know you're extremely resourceful,' he taunted, his temper apparently easing at the sight of her predicament. 'Naturally, you would think of this course of action. As I don't much fancy staying awake to make sure you don't come creeping down to go through my pockets, I think something had better be done about it, don't you?'

To her horror he drew his arm back and threw the keys as far as he could into the racing river, so far, in fact, that she didn't even hear the sound of them hitting the water. She couldn't believe it.

'You've trapped us!' She stared at him wildly. 'We'll have to push the Ferrari out of the way before we can get my car out, and it's all uphill!'

'I'm not anxious to leave,' he assured her smoothly. 'I thought I'd made that quite clear.'

Victoria stared at him for a few more seconds, her mind working frantically, but there was no way out now unless they walked. Thoughts of towing the Ferrari aside with her own car, thoughts of pushing it back across the bridge, thoughts of pushing Damien into the river, all ran through her mind as she glared at him, and he began to laugh softly, his eyes following her frantic machinations with admiration.

'You've come to life, princess!' he said with deep satisfaction. 'Those green eyes are looking as they used to look when you were about fifteen and trying to work out how to get your own way. The cool model has utterly vanished. If nothing else good comes of this, the whole thing will have been worthwhile for that fact alone—just to see you as you used to be.'

'Oh, nothing good will come of it, I can assure you,' Victoria seethed. 'I'm sure that when you and Grandfather worked out exactly how the whole of the firm could be passed to you, he had no idea what a monster you are. He did care about me, after all, and he would never have imagined that you would get me into this sort of situation.'

'You created your own crisis,' he pointed out with mocking logic. 'I never sent you here, I merely joined you, and you were extremely glad to see me last night. You were scared long before I arrived. I can still hear that little gasp of relief as you threw your arms around my neck—"Damien!"—that was very satisfying.' He looked at her scathingly. 'As for the firm, I'll point out yet again that you have your share of it when we get married, it doesn't pass to me ever.'

'No, but I'll have to battle all my life to have something more than a subdued existence!'

'Is that what you imagine being married to me will be like? An existence? Is that how you feel when you're in my arms? It's not how you look, Victoria.'

He was no longer mocking. He was serious, the blue eyes vibrantly intent on her face and she couldn't take any more. She turned and walked into the cottage, leaving him there.

At lunchtime she made very hefty sandwiches and slapped them in front of him. She had been tempted to feed herself only, but he had made breakfast and she was not without feelings of justice. He had found a few musty old books, and appeared to be deeply interested in them, his only comment a quick murmur of thanks. She took her lunch outside to eat, and then began to attack the small bedraggled garden, taking her rage out on the weeds.

Rain drove her indoors. It had been clouding over for an hour, and it came suddenly with no gentle beginning. The raindrops were heavy, and within minutes there was a downpour of astonishing proportions. Victoria dived inside and slammed the door, flustered as she met Damien's slow smile. She didn't need to be told what he was thinking. They were both now trapped indoors in a very small cottage. She turned away and went to wash her hands.

That was another thing! There was no elaborate bathroom here, only the loo was private. She had boiled water and washed in the kitchen before he came, but now the whole idea of having a wash of any sort became a worry. She walked in and sat by the fire, trying to work out how to broach the subject nonchalantly.

There was nothing nonchalant about the atmosphere at all. Damien was reading with total concentration, ignoring her, but he was utterly surrounded by his own atmosphere, an atmosphere he carried around with him.

He was not a man to ignore. Waves of power always radiated from him, and now there was more—an air of waiting. It was about as easy to dismiss him as to dismiss a jungle-cat. She felt as if she were being stalked!

'I want to get a very good wash!' She blurted it out suddenly, after sitting watching him surreptitiously with mounting anxiety.

'Are you inviting me to wash the beautiful back?' he murmured, without looking up.

'The facilities are limited!' she snapped, blushing furiously. 'You'll have noticed that we don't have a bathroom.'

He put the book down and looked up at her steadily.

'You need the kitchen to yourself? You imagine I'm going to break the door down and ravish you?'

He didn't look angry, but there was that certain reprimanding look on his face that threw her right back to her teens. She silently acknowledged that it was insulting to skirt so stealthily around the subject.

'I was just warning you, that's all. I want to get cleaned up now, before I make the dinner.'

'Carry on,' he murmured, going back to his book, and she went upstairs feeling about an inch high and rather childish. It annoyed her. He was always so superior, so self-sufficient. With a wild burst of contrariness she wanted to go back down and start again. She had wanted to sit by him, to sit at his feet, resting against his knee. He made her feel like that. Even though they were here and he had stranded her, there was this ridiculous feeling that she was safe with him.

CHAPTER NINE

SHE was irritated by her own stupidity, and for a while she sat on the end of her bed trying to deal with her nails. Weeding had been a perfectly fruitless way of passing her time. She would be out of here tomorrow somehow! The garden could cover the cottage, for all she cared. It would have been a bit more practical to go and take her annoyance out on the logs.

She gathered her toiletries and went downstairs, her towel and dressing-gown over her arm, her steps coming to a startled halt to find Damien crouching by the fire, pouring water into a huge tin bath.

'Where did you get that tin bath?' she asked in a stupefied voice.

'The shed. Actually, I imagine that it's zinc,' he muttered, giving the sides a sharp rap. He stood and came towards her. 'Your bath awaits you, princess,' he murmured mockingly.

'I—is it for me?'

'You imagine that it's for me? It's cleaned out, filled with warm water, and in the only really warm place there is. We wouldn't want you to catch a cold, would we?'

'It's best not to use too much water, the tank——' It was difficult to find anything to say, and he smiled derisively, listening to the steady downpour outside.

'I think that the one thing we're not going to run out of is water. Don't hang around here, the water in the bath will get cold.'

'Thank you, er—what are you going to——?'

'Not sit and watch you.' His eyes flared over her flushed face with enough scorn to make her blush even more. 'I intend to have my scrub in the kitchen. You can call me when you're ready, and then I'll empty this bath for you.'

'It—it's cold in the kitchen.'

'You're inviting me to join you?' The black brows raised ironically. 'I don't think that would be a good idea, not after this morning. I'll stick to the kitchen, but don't linger or I'll get impatient.'

He picked up his travelling bag and simply walked out. Victoria hurried forward and began, rather fearfully, to undress. How was it that he managed to make her feel guilty, as if she had hurt him by pulling away from him this morning? He acted as if Heather didn't exist at all, his mind compartmentalised to suit himself.

The water was just right, and with a bit of careful manoeuvering she was able to sit and still be able to wash. It seemed the height of luxury. The thought of the bathroom in her flat with its cool tiles, the antiseptic cleanliness, the easy access to modern requirements, faded into nothing compared with this.

Damien had built up the fire, and the light flickered round the old room. This was what it must have been like for the workers at the mill when her great-grandfather had first built the cottages to house them. Now the houses were much sought after, modernised, functional. They didn't know what they were missing!

'Have you got warm water, Damien?' She called out loudly to be heard above the noise of the rain. She suddenly felt cosy, close to him.

'I'm not as delicate as you, my pet! Don't let your conscience trouble you.' There was the same old mockery in his voice, but she realised with surprise that she wasn't annoyed. It was comforting to be able to have this warm luxury and shout out to Damien through the door. It made her flat seem more cold and unreal than ever. If she were married to Damien...

She wanted to stay dreamily by the fire, but the thought of Damien becoming impatient and getting annoyed made her hurry. She didn't want him to be annoyed. He had been either annoyed or mocking since she had first come home. He had always been either annoyed or mocking, except for a little while. She had never felt able to be warmly close to him, it was all wishful thinking. The reality of things took away the warmth, and wiped the slight smile from her face.

She would always be lonely if she married Damien. There would always be a hungry need to get close to him, to feel loved and not merely wanted. He had always made her feel lonely because, even when she had been eighteen and he had set out to enchant her, it had all been so much manipulation. There had never been warmth or love. She had wanted him to adore her, her dreams wistful ones where his face lit up with joy at the sight of her. It had never happened, and it never would.

She got out of the bath and dried herself, slipping into her dressing-gown and tying the belt tightly.

'I'm ready!' She called out in a dull voice, all the pleasure faded, and he opened the door and walked in. He was gleamingly clean, a white high-necked sweater contrasting sharply with his black hair, jeans fitting snugly to his strong legs.

'The water went cold?' he enquired.

'No, it was all very nice, thank you.' She avoided his eyes and he walked over slowly, standing to look down at her.

'You could have lingered a while. I already started the dinner.'

'I had my bath. I'll cook the dinner.'

It was suddenly painful not to have that hard hand on her arm. His old habits seemed to have deserted him and, contrarily, she missed the things she had complained of: his possessive, iron grip, the way he tilted her face with that imperious finger. Now he just stood looking down at her, and she wanted him to touch her in any way at all.

'What's the matter?'

'Nothing. I'll get dressed and come down to help with the meal.' She spun round and walked out, her heart beating painfully as she realised that she had felt so ready to throw her arms around his waist and bury her head against him, to beg to be loved. She was an idiot!

When she got back downstairs he had already disposed of the bath, and they worked together silently to make a meal. It was a painful silence to Victoria, but Damien simply worked steadily and ignored her. He built up the fire and they ate in front of it, their plates on small tables as they sat facing each other in front of the roaring blaze.

'Do you think it's going to stop raining?'

The downpour had not eased at all, and it was beginning to take on a rather menacing sound. She wanted Damien to reassure her, and his rather distant aura brought her to the point of asking outright what he felt.

'Eventually, I imagine.'

'It's never even stopped for a minute since this afternoon!' she reminded him crossly, annoyed at his laconic reply. 'This is an island in the middle of a really fast-moving river.'

'If you want me to build an ark, just say so,' he murmured and went right on ignoring her.

'You'll probably get up in the morning to find your car submerged!' she snapped.

'I doubt it.'

'We're trapped here!'

'Don't you like being trapped with me in this wilderness?' He looked up with quietly mocking eyes. 'This is the sort of place that brings people together.'

'It's more likely to drive me to violence!'

'Hard to imagine,' he murmured, and to her annoyance he picked up the book he had been reading and totally ignored her.

She sprang up and cleared the plates, storming off into the kitchen to wash up, and then going up to bed with no further word to him. He was reading in the lamplight. Let him damage his eyes! What did she care?

In spite of everything, though, she felt more secure with him downstairs, and she fell asleep almost at once, even though the drumming of the rain sounded louder than ever.

The loud crash of thunder woke her, and she sat up in bed instantly. She was not afraid of storms. All her life she had been used to the sound of the storms that raged over the wild moorland. She was not, however, accustomed to the persistent torrential rain that now seemed to be heavier than usual.

She lay back down, pulling the covers to her ears, but her mind began to wander over the possibilities. They were, after all, in the middle of a river—a wide river. When she had arrived here the water had looked deep and fast-flowing. What was it like now? She had never been too happy about deep water—even a swimming pool was not her idea of fun, and her mind pictured the black, swirling water that surrounded the little house. Had it crept up higher? How long before this minuscule island was flooded?

That it had been here for so long did not make things safe at all. It might have been flooded in the past, submerged. She got out of bed and crept to the window, but it was pitch black, and then, in the flash of brilliant lightning, she saw the racing river, the raging water, and her heart leapt uncomfortably when she imagined that it was much closer to the house.

She made for the door, going out and creeping downstairs. Damien had a torch, she had seen it close to his travelling bag. With that she could really see.

She almost fell over him. She had imagined that he had accepted the bed-settee as it was, but he was thorough in everything, and the uncomfortable-looking object was fully opened into a bed. It was taking up a great deal of space.

Feeling very nervous at this unexpected obstacle, she edged her way around it. There was still a warm-looking glow from the fire and, after the utter blackness of her room, it was quite easy to see. Down here the river was louder than ever, and she searched carefully until she found the big torch she had seen earlier.

As her fingers closed round it, Damien's fingers closed round her own.

'Oh!' She jumped and tried to pull away, but he held her hand fast.

'What exactly are you looking for?' He sounded very dangerous in the dim light, and he didn't even bother to sit up. His arm was outstretched to grasp her, his face still not visible.

'I—I wanted the torch!'

'You're hardly dressed for escape.' He sat up slowly, resting on his elbow, the firelight a red glow on the broad expanse of his chest. His eyes moved over her slender figure, fragile and vulnerable in the shift she wore. 'What are you up to?'

'I—I wanted to turn the torch on the river. It's too loud!' She could hear the faint panic in her voice, and so could he.

'Scared?' he asked softly.

'I don't like deep water.'

'You're not in deep water,' he murmured sardonically, and she tried to pull the torch free. His hand only tightened on hers.

'Please let me look, Damien,' she asked in a low voice. 'I have to see what it's like!'

She could see his eyes on her now, their steady glance making her feel a trifle foolish, but she felt no less afraid.

'I'll look.' He sat up and swung his legs out of bed, and for one giddy moment she thought he was wearing nothing at all, but he had pyjama trousers on—black ones—and he was standing beside her, towering over her, the torch in his hand before she could recover from her shock.

She stared at him a little wildly, and he looked utterly exasperated as he moved around the bed and made for the door. A great gust of wind blew the rain in and he stepped clear of it with an irritated murmur, but, even so, he turned the powerful torch towards the river and then closed the door.

She still looked worried, and his eyes narrowed on her with even more irritation.

'I don't suppose you'll sleep until you've seen for yourself. You'd better have a quick look.'

She knew he was quietly furious with her. She also knew that this was probably childish, but she had to look, he was quite right. She moved to the door, and he opened it and handed her the torch. The white beam cut through the darkness and she focused it on the river's edge. It had risen a little, but not much at all.

'Satisfied?'

'Yes, thank you.'

He closed the door and locked it, and she found it very difficult to move away from him.

'Now what?'

The same exasperation was in his voice, but it did not make her hurry back upstairs. He was strong and capable, like a giant in the firelight, and she had to clench her hands to stop them from reaching out to touch him. She wanted to rest against the strength of his chest, to feel herself swept up into his arms.

Her eyes wandered over his skin, and she found her hands coming up towards him. She clutched them against her face, powerless to simply put them down again by her sides.

'Oh, no!' he said harshly. 'Once in a day is quite enough to be tied into knots inside. What's the plan this time? Do you get into bed with me and then slide out again? Apart from the obvious danger to you, I don't fancy it!'

The contempt just seemed to wash right over her, and he stood staring down into her eyes until she lowered her head to shut out the scorn that seemed to fill his face. She was humiliated and shaken.

'All right!' He put the torch down and then lifted her, his arm beneath her legs, and she made no protest at all. After all, he had read her mind. She wanted exactly this, to be close to him. Danger didn't matter when it was Damien.

'Why did you come downstairs?' He slid her into the warmth he had just left, coming in beside her and resting on his elbow to look down at her.

'I—I told you. I'm afraid of deep water.'

'More afraid than you are of me? Why do I find myself in this delightful situation? Is it something too difficult to be without? You've been back to London after all. Were you too busy hiding to risk going back to your...?'

She lashed out at him, tears of humiliation on her face, and he caught her wrist tightly, anticipating the slap and grasping her with iron cruelty.

'So you were lonely up those dark stairs?' he derided. 'You'll be just as lonely here, because I don't intend to help out at all.'

'I don't need *you*!'

She didn't mean to sound so distraught, but it sounded like that and she looked away rapidly.

'Oh, I believe you. Is there somebody special in London, or does it have to be someone from the bright lights—anyone?'

She wanted to say yes, anything to pay him back for the cruelly relentless insults, but she turned her head away, trying to summon up the sheer courage it would take to move away from him.

'You're wrong about me, Damien. One day you'll——'

'You beautiful little liar,' he said softly. 'Do you think I can't feel it when you're close? You were at school in London, and you couldn't wait to get back down there.'

She couldn't answer back this time. She was choked with tears, hurt as she had never been, and he slid down in the bed, turning away from her.

'Goodnight, Victoria.'

Why did he think the things he thought? Nobody had ever touched her. Her cold beauty put them off and, even if it hadn't, she was utterly without trust, too afraid to take any sort of chance. Damien had always been at the back of her mind—more often than not at the very front of it too.

What did she want to do after all? There was no need to dig deeply for an answer. She wanted to be with Damien. She always had. The tears fell down her cheeks, and she tried to stifle the choking sobs that rose to the surface. Now she dared not move or he would know. She turned with her back to him, curling up desperately, unable to contain the sound of misery that was torn from her as her control was lost and the sobs took over.

She sat up to get out of bed, the position of the bed-settee making it necessary to actually climb over him, her body shaken with the force of her tears.

'Stay.' His voice was as dark as the night, and she stopped half over him, her face wet with tears in the darkness.

'Stay with me,' he said softly, as he pulled her down to him.

She was too filled with aching unhappiness to struggle as he lowered her on top of him; her face came to his shoulder and his arms wrapped around her in the darkness.

'You feel like heaven,' he murmured. 'Slender and trembling, long silky legs against mine. Don't cry. I don't want to hear you cry.'

He was speaking so gently and it seemed to linger in her head, making her warm and soft as her arms wound around his neck, her tear-wet face against his chest.

'That's better.' His head bent and found her lips in the dim light, his mouth opening at her shuddering response, and she stretched out over him, almost weightless as his hands moved over her, shaping her from her shoulders to her thighs with slow, lingering caresses that moulded her to him.

'How is this to end?' he whispered against her lips, his hands restless on her slender flanks, and she raised herself to look down into his face. The fire's glow was still there and she could see him clearly. A log fell in the old grate and the room was suddenly brighter, the flickering shadows dancing across the softened planes of his face.

'Tell me?' His eyes were brilliantly blue in the firelight, and all her love came back with one wild rush as she bent her head and found his lips with hers, her hand against the smooth rasp of his skin, a low murmur of pain in her throat.

'Victoria!' His lips out-matched hers, and his restless hands slid beneath the skimpy shift to find her skin, to move urgently against her smooth back and waist, and to plunge again to her thighs as his body surged against hers.

'Before the flames die, before everything goes dark, I want to see you.' He pulled the shift over her head, but instantly her lips found his again, frustrating him when he wished to see the beauty he had uncovered, and he lifted her by the waist until she was above him, her silken hair fallen around her face, her breasts high and full as his eyes moved over her.

He lowered her slowly until the sharp peaks of her breasts brushed against the crisp black hair that covered his chest, his eyes on hers as she shuddered at the tingling shock of pleasure, and then he clasped her against him with a low groan.

'Tell me to stop, and I'll stop right now,' he breathed against her lips as she murmured frantically, totally given up to the desire that raged inside her, her skin burning as it touched his. 'But don't leave it for one minute more, or there'll be no stopping.'

Her feverish little cries were wild, almost loud, and he turned her swiftly, shrugging out of the last of his garments and moving to her at once.

'Then let me look at all of you,' he whispered thickly, 'because all of you is what I want, every beat of your heart, every thought in your mind, every beautiful inch of you.'

She closed her eyes as he drew back the covering, his hand tracing her body as he looked at her. There was only the crackling of the fire, the driving rain and the harsh unsteady sound of their breathing.

'How shall I take you?' he asked thickly. 'Wildly and quickly with the ferocity that comes of years of waiting, years of watching you and wanting you, or slowly and gently, in case your gauzy butterfly-wings crush and disappear?'

'Damien!' His power frightened her. The desire in his voice was edged with anger; her eyes opened wide as he hovered over her, and he smiled that slow smile that tore at her heart.

'You don't want to marry me, and I know it,' he said huskily. 'But you want me, and I know that too because, if you hadn't, your fear would have driven you straight back to your bed—it would never have allowed you to come to me. When you did that, it was all over. You've stopped running now, haven't you, Victoria?'

'Yes.' She could only whisper, and her breath was a mere gasp in her throat as his head bent to the tight arousal of her breast, his hands hard and possessive on her as he took the rosy peak between his teeth, and then soothingly into the warmth of his mouth.

Rapture flooded through her as he moved over her, kissing every part of her hungrily, her name almost frenzied on his lips until he drew her beneath him, parting her thighs and lifting her towards him.

'You belong to me,' he murmured against her mouth. 'You always have. I told you long ago, but you left me. I'll never let you leave me again, Victoria!'

There was a possessive anger deep down inside him, and she knew that he believed all he had said about her life in London. It wasn't just some way to scorn her. It was like acid, eating away at him, assuring him that his past suspicions of her were only too correct. Even now, her eagerness was convincing him that she was far from innocent, and a wave of panic hit her as she felt the power of his body over her own.

'Damien!' He mistook the plea in her voice and his lips covered hers, drowning the cry of pain as he possessed her fiercely.

Her whole body shook with the force of it, her nails raking into his back, her legs rigid with shock, and he raised his head, his eyes no longer dark and dazed, but vividly blue against the flush of his skin.

'Oh, hell!'

He was completely still, his gaze disbelieving as he watched tears fill her eyes and slowly roll down her cheeks.

'Victoria.' He whispered her name, and she felt his whole being withdraw from her.

'Don't leave me!' Her sharp cry stopped him, as her hands clutched his shoulders.

'I've hurt you badly.' His voice was filled with anger, but she could face that.

'Not as badly as you'll hurt me if you leave me,' she sobbed.

'Do you think I'm a savage?' he asked in a shaken voice. 'Is that how you've always seen me? Do you think I would have trapped you here if I'd known? Wanting you doesn't give me the right to take you like that. Why didn't you tell me?'

'I did. I—I tried to. Y-you never believe me.' She was crying quietly, the pain fading as he held her gently, and her arms wound around his neck as she buried her face against his shoulder. 'Don't go away from me, Damien! Don't leave me. I'm so unhappy.'

He swallowed hard at the broken sound of her voice, the harsh tension leaving his body as he eased her face back into the glow of firelight.'

'Come here.' He wrapped her in his arms, his lips catching the falling tears. 'I won't hurt you again.' He looked down at her gently, and then gathered her tenderly close. 'Oh, Vicky! Vicky!' he whispered.

He kissed her gently over and over, until her tight muscles relaxed and the panic eased from her body. The warmth grew slowly, and he stroked her face with a slow tenderness, his lips moving over her neck and shoulders as he held her closely, and her breathing slowed too, from the panic-stricken shallow breaths to deep relaxing waves, that allowed warmth to flood through her.

The reality of his nearness grew with every second. She was locked close to Damien, part of him, belonging to him as she had never belonged to anyone, and her fingers threaded in his black hair as she lifted her mouth to his, moving against him in a timid way that had him pulling her closer still.

'Don't be frightened,' he murmured, as he began to move gently inside her. The gasp that left her lips was without any fear, as a deep wonder grew that spread through her whole body, and lifted her away from the quiet room where the fire died from flickering flames to a dim glow.

There were more flames inside her than had ever been in the fire, a drumming in her ears that silenced the heavy rain, as Damien took her out of the world for timeless, throbbing minutes, his voice deep and shaken against her lips.

'Vicky, you're so beautiful. You'll never know how much I've wanted you!'

She was liquid and molten, lost in a velvet cloud and the burning blue of his eyes, her lips whispering his name with frenzied pleas as his mouth fused with hers, and the whole world rocked about them.

Drifting back to earth was not the cold thing she had half dreaded. For seconds she fought against it, clinging to him, calling his name.

'I'm here!' His hand cupped her face, his eyes blazing down at her, and then his lips covered hers again in a deep, drugging kiss that held her fast until she was safely back in the silent room.

'Damien...'

As he released her she wanted to speak to him, to tell him that it didn't matter about the hurt, but he would not allow it.

'No! No words!' he ordered, moving away and taking her in his arms to lie quietly beside him. 'Right now I don't want words—certainly not words said when you're still shaken by two experiences that have altered your world.'

'I'm not a child,' she whispered tremulously.

'Oh, I can vouch for that!' he assured her, his quick laugh harsh and bitter. It chilled her and she moved quickly, wanting to escape from any harsh feelings.

'I'll go back to bed.'

'You're in bed,' he assured her, tightening his arms around her. 'You came to my bed willingly, and you'll stay permanently, wherever my bed happens to be. You belong to me, Victoria.'

The tears had lingered on her face and his fingers wiped them away slowly, his eyes meeting hers.

'I'll never let you cry again,' he said quietly, pulling her head to his shoulder.

She wondered how he was going to make that happen. There was Heather and there was only desire, but the arms that held her were secure and strong, and even now his fingers were lightly brushing her skin, as if deep down in him there was a protectiveness that was almost gentle.

'Damien——'

'Go to sleep, Victoria,' he ordered softly, and he turned her towards him, holding her tightly until she curled up against him and began to drift into a deep sleep. She thought he kissed her forehead, but when she murmured his name, he didn't answer.

It was noise that awakened her and, for a second, she lay looking at the beamed ceiling, puzzled that the noise seemed to be coming from there. She was not at all disorientated. She knew where she was, and she knew that Damien was no longer beside her. The rain had stopped, and the sunlight was trying to penetrate the room through the closed curtains. It was morning and she had been in Damien's arms all night.

She felt different, a little bruised, a small pain inside her that made her feel very vulnerable, and a growing uneasiness when she realised that Damien was not there and that the noise was coming from her bedroom.

He came downstairs and looked into the room, coming in when he saw she was awake and the sight of her bedding, neatly folded and slung over his arm, had her eyes anxiously on him. She couldn't speak, though. Now, in the light of day, he was Damien again: powerful, dangerous and hurtful. She avoided his eyes and he came to the bed to look down at her.

'I woke you up?' he asked quietly. 'You would have had to be awake soon, in any case.' He sat on the edge of the bed. 'How do you feel?'

'Perfectly all right. I'll get up if you'll——' She suddenly realised that her shift was lying across the bed, and that only the sheets kept her from his eyes.

'Stay there. I'll make you a cup of tea.'

He left at once and she reached for her shift, struggling into it, every part of her aching, her legs trembling as she stood. She had to sit on the edge of the bed for a moment, and he must have had the kettle boiling already, because he was back before she had in any way recovered from the effort of getting up.

'I thought I told you to stay put.' He towered over her, in no way like a lover, and her pale face flushed with embarrassment.

'I have to get dressed.'

'You have to stay right there and drink your tea.' His eyes moved over her, pausing in shock as he saw the bruises on her arms and legs. 'Hell!'

He stared at her for a minute, and she felt so flustered that she didn't know what to say, except to blurt out rapidly, 'I bruise easily.'

It was not the best thing to have said. His face looked even more grim, and a flare of colour stained his cheekbones as he strode out and shut the door. She stared miserably into her tea, not at all sure what to do after she had drunk it. What was he thinking? Just how much was he berating himself this morning? She had started it all, and she knew there was no way he would ever let her escape now. She didn't want to, either. Just the brief spell back in London had shown her what life would be without him, and whatever she had to face she would face it, so long as she could see Damien all the time, so long as she could be with him.

He came back in as she was finishing her drink, and evidently he had recovered from his bitter anger. At any rate, he was more gentle.

'I've got all your bedding down here. I haven't packed for you, because I didn't know what you'd need to use first. If you feel like getting dressed and then shouting down to me, I'll come and pack for you.'

'Are we leaving?'

'What do you think?' he asked harshly. 'Another night like that would probably finish both of us off!'

She didn't know exactly what he meant, but he was determined to go, and she nodded almost absently, her mind not quite yet her own. He would be even more angry when he came to have to try and move his car.

She walked to the stairs, feeling suddenly quite lethargic as she faced the thought of the steep flight, and she only knew he had followed her when he swung her up into his arms and carried her up the stairs.

'Damien! I'm perfectly capable of seeing to myself,' she said, misery sharpening her voice as he placed her carefully on her feet inside her room. 'I've not become an invalid just because I'm no longer——'

She stopped in embarrassment, cursing the tongue that sometimes ran away with her. It would have been as well not to remind him of that.

'You look shaken and distressed,' he said in a low voice. 'It's a new experience for me.'

She assumed that it was. Heather was no innocent!

'Then you don't treat all your women like invalids?' she said nastily, jealousy tearing into her at the implication of his remarks.

'No!' he grated, his face suddenly pale. 'I don't normally savage delicate little virgins!' He grabbed her and hauled her against him, wrapping her in his arms and staring wildly at her. 'I don't normally feel like doing it all over again the next day either.'

Before she could quite take that in, his lips covered hers, and she could feel the shaken anger in him, the tight control that stiffened his whole body. He let her go abruptly and turned to the door.

'Get dressed!' he snapped. 'As you're so well recovered you can pack your things. I'll get everything out to the car, and don't try to carry your cases down these stairs or I'll probably beat you. You'll have even more bruises then!'

He went downstairs much too quickly, and she looked round in a daze trying to decide what to wear, wondering how she was going to get a wash, wondering how he was going to get them out of here.

She had never expected to feel like this after a night in Damien's arms. Her whole world was upside down and, from the look of him, so was his. The thought of going back home came creeping into her mind, but she thrust it out with a frightened speed. The here and now was quite enough to cope with. Wearily she dressed, and then went dutifully down after she had packed. It was unwise to consider antagonising him further.

He went out to the car with some of the things, and she hastily washed her face in cold water, not bothering with any make-up. The effort was too much and, in any case, he was moving like a whirlwind and she felt the need to help. He had finished off the whole of downstairs while she had been dressing, and she began to gather things to take out to the car.

'Sit there!' He came in, removed the things she was carrying and pushed her to the chair. 'Move when I tell you, and not before. I'll get your cases!'

He was stiffly angry, and she decided to do exactly as she was told for now. To annoy him further would only make matters worse, and they were bad enough now. Damien was back in his place—a god who walked on a different path, a cold, hard force that held her spellbound. The man who had held her so tenderly the night before and told her not to cry had disappeared as if he had never been.

He called her when everything was packed, and she moved to the door reluctantly.

'Sorry to be leaving?' The derision was there again, and she avoided the blue eyes that had noted her reluctance.

'No. I hate this place!' His cold attitude made her feel lost, and she felt like lashing out at him.

'I can imagine!'

He walked out to the car, leaving her to lock the door and put the heavy key in her bag. She should be sad to leave, her mind told her, as her eyes moved over the cottage and then the fast-moving river. Here in this place she had spent the night in Damien's arms, but there was no lingering magic. How could there be?

He was watching her as she turned, and she hastily blinked tears away, her expression changing from sadness to astonishment as she saw that he had the door of the Ferrari open, all the things piled inside.

'We'll have to get your car back,' he said coolly, 'so you follow me very closely. I want to be able to see you in the driving mirror all the time.' She just nodded. There was no way that she was going to try and escape again.

'How are you going to get your car out?' she asked, and he thought she was stupid apparently, because he simply dangled keys from his fingers and prepared to get into the car.

Fury rose unexpectedly, as she realised that he had always had two sets of keys. The great gesture of tossing them into the river had been nothing more than a trick!

'Y-you let me think that we were stranded here? You let me suffer all that anxiety?' Her voice was brittle with rage. 'All that for a mere gesture?'

'I hadn't intended that you should suffer so much!' he said tightly. 'I certainly hadn't expected you to suffer as you did last night. I was simply tired of chasing you!'

She stared at him in silence, and then blazed at him with all the humiliation and worries at the top of her mind.

'I hate you, Damien!' she raged. 'I've always hated you. You've never done anything in your life to make me change my mind, and this little interlude has been the most despicable thing of all!'

'I don't have to be told that,' he assured her coldly. 'I'm well aware of the most despicable thing I've done. I'm not likely ever to forget it.' He got into his car and it started first time, its low growl like Damien, angry and dangerous, like an untamed creature.

He reversed with frightening speed, and then pulled up slightly beyond the bridge to watch her drive over. She didn't look back at the cottage—she didn't need to, it would stay in her mind always.

CHAPTER TEN

AT THE first town they reached Damien pulled into a hotel, and she followed without a word as he went inside and ordered breakfast. He left her for a few minutes, and when he came back he asked for her car keys.

'Why?' She looked suspicious, and his lips tightened angrily.

'I've arranged for it to be left here. I've also arranged for it to be collected and driven to London. It's a long way to drive, and I'd like you to rest.'

'I'm perfectly capable of driving,' she said wearily.

'No, you're not. I know how you feel.'

'Oh, no, you don't, Damien!' she said bitterly. 'You don't know at all how I feel! Someone with a total belief in their own power could never know how an ordinary person feels.'

'Just give me the keys!' he ordered tersely, his imperious hand outstretched. 'You're sitting with me in comfort, however you feel.'

'If it eases your conscience.'

She dropped the keys into his hand, and pushed her meal aside. She felt sick and shaken, her head aching badly. She went to the powder-room, and when she came out he was waiting, his own breakfast untouched. He led her to his car without a word, and as they reached the main roads the beautiful car showed its speed, as Damien let it race northwards, his face grim and distant.

It was dark when they reached the valley. After a stop for a very silent meal, they had come straight through, but it was a long journey no matter what car was racing along the motorway, and many lights were out as they drove along the valley road and then climbed the hill to Damien's house.

He hadn't spoken all the way, and neither had Victoria, but now he seemed to almost hear her growing anxiety.

'Molly's here,' he said quietly. 'I asked her to come and be housekeeper, and she agreed.'

'What about that woman who——'

'Mrs Randle left,' he said shortly, and she didn't press the matter any further. She hadn't been in this house for years—not since Damien's parents had died—and she had been rather dreading the thought of coping with the grim woman who had kept house for Damien and Joel since then.

'What did you tell Molly?'

'Nothing. It's not my habit to go around explaining myself to people. She was staying at her sister's, as you told me, and I simply went to find her and offered her the job.'

'Will Joel be awake?'

'He's away,' Damien told her shortly. 'He'll be back tomorrow afternoon, all being well.'

No, it would not be well, she was sure of that. She was shivering in the cold moorland wind as he stopped the car and helped her out, and she prepared herself by taking a few deep breaths. Another old house to face, another grim reminder of the past, when tyrannical men grew rich in this valley and their women reared children and sat in calm-faced respectability. The aura of her grandfather was all about her. As usual, he had won— and so had Damien.

The house was a complete shock. She knew this house. She had known it all her life. It was almost identical to the one on the opposite hillside, the house she had called home. This, though, was different. Since his parents had died it was clear that Damien had taken control here as he took control everywhere. It had been transformed.

Her grandfather had stuck to tradition, and it had been
only the truth when one of the women at the mill had
surmised that the big old house had been lonely. There
was an oppressive atmosphere about the place she had
been brought up in, but there was none of that here. It
was light and airy, the whole place modern, only the size
of the rooms any reminder that this was a Victorian
house. She followed Damien into the huge drawing-room
that had once been filled with the same type of furniture
that she now owned, a memory of dark walls, dark
carpets and curtains in her mind. Now it was bright,
lamp-lit and comfortable.

Two long white settees flanked the fireplace, a pale
green carpet covered the wide expanse of floor—only
the most beautiful of the old pieces had been kept and
the whole blended perfectly.

'You—you've altered everything!' She was hard
pressed to recognise more than the odd piece of furniture.

'Not personally, I do assure you,' he murmured drily.
'I had a whole team of interior designers in the house.
I don't much care for Victoriana. Bric-a-brac and pic-
tures of the ancestors are not my style.'

'Grandfather clung to the old things,' she said quietly,
and he glanced across at her.

'Yes, he was a stubborn man. I don't count dis-
comfort a virtue. Tomorrow you can let me know what
you think of the whole place. For now, though, I think
bed is indicated.'

The way he said it brought a blush to her cheeks, and
she looked round in a flustered manner, trying to locate
her bag as Damien watched her with sardonic eyes.

'I'll bring up your luggage in a few minutes,' he said
wryly. 'You'll want to get changed. If Molly is still up,
I'll get her to bring you a hot drink.'

'I can take care of myself!' He had a way of making
her feel childish with a few well-chosen words.

'Can you?' he enquired sarcastically, following her into the hall and making for the front door and the car. 'I've seen no great evidence of it.'

She was sitting on the bed, looking around at the comfortable and rather luxurious room, when Damien called out and walked in. He had too many suitcases to knock, and she got up to stand watching him warily as he put the cases down.

'You're perfectly safe!' he assured her irascibly as he caught sight of her expression. 'I'm not about to insist upon spending the night with you.'

He turned and walked out as Molly came in with a hot drink, and Victoria made a great effort to smile. She felt more lonely than she had ever felt, and Molly's presence didn't help at all. She wanted Damien. She wanted to be wrapped in his arms, hearing him tell her that he loved her. An impossible dream.

He had gone before she got up the next morning. She had been left to sleep, and she was so exhausted that she slept until almost ten o'clock. Molly hovered over her as she ate breakfast, and then she was left to explore the house and the newly laid-out gardens. It seemed that, with the alterations, Damien had wiped out the past here, the good with the bad. There was not even a memory of Joel—even the garden where they had spent so much of their time was obliterated. It made him seem so distant and unapproachable.

She remembered Dale's key and went upstairs to write him a quick note of thanks. She was just sealing the envelope when there was a brief knock on her door. She thought it was Molly and called out as cheerfully as possible, but when the door was opened it was Joel, his face still and watchful as she sprang up to face him.

'So big brother brought you back?' he said quietly, his eyes on her pale face. 'You don't look too good. Did he have to beat you up to get you here?'

She stood there shaking her head, not knowing at all what his attitude was. In many ways he was like Damien, she realised. It was not at all surprising, but she had never noticed it until lately.

'I wouldn't give much for either of you,' he continued softly, still standing in the doorway. 'Damien's down at the works looking like death too. It's not helping matters that he's trying to break in a new secretary, who seems to have made a rare muddle of things while we've both been away.'

'What—what about Heather?'

'Oh, Heather got the big push. I was there at the tail-end of that before Damien took off after you. He was dismissing her—quietly. Damien at his worst. I got the shivers just hearing the end of it.'

Yes, she knew Damien at his worst. His silence was always a trifle menacing. To be told off quietly would be fairly traumatic if it was Damien who was doing it. She was unable to take in the implication of Heather's dismissal. She had no real idea of what it meant.

'He normally shouts at me,' she said, almost vaguely, and for the first time a smile grew on Joel's face.

'Me, too! We must be privileged.' He walked in further, and then looked at her with a smile that contained his old affection. 'I'm sorry about the outburst the last time I saw you, Vic. I was furious with Damien, and utterly confused. It's not much of an excuse, but it's all I can come up with.'

'It's all right. I—I wouldn't want to stop being a friend.'

'More than a friend—a sister-in-law!' he corrected wryly. His face softened at her quick look of anxiety. 'I was miles across the moors before your last words rang in my head and sank in. I should have known you loved him. A few years ago it was fairly obvious. I thought you'd grown out of it.'

'It's not something you grow out of,' Victoria said softly, her eyes downcast. 'It stays with you like—like——'

'Like a broken nose, to put life and Damien into context,' he said with a wide grin, and her heart lifted as she looked up and met smiling eyes. 'Welcome home, Vic,' he said, walking across and hugging her close. She smiled up into his eyes, and he bent to kiss her cheek.

'Touching!'

Damien's caustic voice had Victoria jumping guiltily.

'All pals again, I see. Shall I look for your bicycles?'

'Now, that's an idea, Vic!' Joel said drily, not at all abashed by Damien's quiet fury. 'I'll get us a couple of bikes, and we'll retrace our old tracks. Being bigger, we can go further now.' He kissed her cheek again and walked out, with a grin at Damien that was not returned.

'Well, you obviously need him,' Damien said coldly, his eyes on her flushed face. 'The last time I saw you, you looked as if you were at death's door, and now look at you—all rosy and bright.'

'I'm happy to have Joel back as a friend.'

He was just as he had always been, domineering, scathing. 'When we're married I'll have a couple of badges made. Joel can have the one marked "friend", mine will say "husband". I wouldn't want you to become confused.'

'I'll never be confused!' she bit out, hurt and weary. 'Joel's the one who cares about me. It's easy to tell the difference.'

He glared at her frustratedly.

'Yes! I'm the one who's marrying you to get my hands on a tradition! I should be quite easy to pick out. I'm the one who hurt you badly, too. It will make me all too recognisable, but, however much he cares about you, I'm going to go on feeling savage every time I see my brother in your room, and you in his arms!'

'He—he came to say he was sorry.'

'And how nicely he says it! Do the kisses get stronger the more sorry he becomes?'

She didn't answer and, for a moment, he stared down at her furiously.

'When you've gathered yourself together, come downstairs to the study. I've got something for you. After that, we'll have coffee together and fix the wedding date.'

'It—it will take time,' she said breathlessly.

'No.' He smiled down at her grimly. 'I've had a special licence for a long time. I'm not waiting. If anyone wants to visit you in a bedroom they're going to find me there, too. You'll not be in this one for long. Make the most of it!'

If there was a forbidding room in this house now, she thought as she went to Damien's study, this was it. It wasn't the room itself, though, it was the very forbidding presence of Damien. He was waiting for her and, although she had hurried, he gave the impression that he had been waiting for a very long time. It only added to her feeling of nervousness.

He stood by his desk looking at her as she shut the door, and she had to admit that, in spite of her love for him, this was a little like an interview with a very irate headmaster. She had no idea what he wanted to give her.

'Come here, Victoria.' He watched her steadily as she came towards him, and then took her hand, looking down at her before he spoke. 'I've had this for a long time,' he said quietly. He slid a ring on her finger, closing his hand around it before she could even see. 'To be exact, I've had it for over six years.'

He opened his hand, and she was able to see the heavy engagement ring he had placed on her finger. It was an emerald, and the way it was cut, the setting, in fact everything about it, told her that this had been bought with the pendant he had given her so long ago, the one she had thrown back at him, the one she had called a 'bond of slavery'.

Her eyes went swiftly to his face, but there was no expression there to tell her he was feeling anything at all.

'It—it's very beautiful,' she murmured, with a trace of desperation in her voice. 'It fits perfectly.'

It was very difficult to keep the sound of tears from her voice. Suddenly she wanted to cry—to cry on Damien's shoulder. All the love that had been hidden for so long was at this moment too much to bear. The way he had given the ring to her, coldly, politely, was so fitting for the type of marriage they would have. It would have pleased their forebears so well.

'I don't want you to take it off ever!' he ordered tightly, and she looked up at him again.

'I won't.'

For a moment there was a flare of some deep emotion on his face, but there was no trace of love.

In spite of his remarks about her friendship with Joel, Damien showed no resentment during the following days. They were all living in the same house, Damien and Joel had work to discuss, and it seemed that everything was going on as usual. Victoria was just an addition to the smoothly running household, as she had once been almost an addition when she was a child.

'Have you seen this?'

Molly came in one morning towards the end of the week, and showed Victoria the local paper. There was an announcement of the engagement, photographs of both Damien and herself, and Victoria was suddenly silent, grateful that Molly went off and left her alone.

Once she had dreamed of this, imagined there would such an announcement. She remembered looking at the paper when she was just eighteen, and day-dreaming that the announcement was about herself and Damien. Now it seemed to be more unreal than it had been then. Damien never came near her. Since the time he had placed the ring on her finger, there had been no close contact with him whatsoever. She might have been marrying a stranger.

She looked up and he was there, watching her stricken face, his eyes flashing to the paper, and he just turned and walked out. When evening came he announced that he had too much work to go to dinner at the local hotel, and waved them out indifferently when Joel offered to take Victoria. Apparently he was not even jealous now that she was here and the wedding assured.

Later, Victoria could not settle to sleep. She tried to read and then gave it up, contenting herself with simply pacing about her room. It was now one week to the wedding. Everything was arranged except that she had not yet bought a wedding dress. Damien had never asked about it. Now it was settled his indifference was frightening. Had it been anyone but Damien she would have thought he had changed his mind.

She looked up, startled, as Damien knocked and came into the room.

'I saw your light,' he said bleakly. 'I need to talk to you, Victoria.' His eyes held hers for a moment, his expression bleak. He looked almost wounded and she felt a burst of alarm about why he had come.

'I've been busy this week, having this drawn up—my solicitor conferring with Gresham and so forth.' He paused and looked at her with unsmiling intensity. 'It was my intention to give you this on the day we were married, but I think it would be perhaps better to give it to you now.'

He handed her a very legal-looking document, and she took it with no real thought of what she did. There was something about him that was subtly different, and anxiety continued to wash over her at the businesslike way he was behaving.

'What is it?'

He frowned a trifle impatiently as he saw that she was not about to read the closely written sheets. 'You must read it for yourself, but I'll give you the gist of it for now, if you like. The document is a deed—a deed to Kendal and Hunt. There was nothing I could do about Andrew's will. It stands. You get your share when you're thirty, or when you marry me.'

He walked over to the window and drew the curtain aside, looking out over the valley. It was not possible to see the names from this side as it had been so easy to see them from her grandfather's house, but even here the red glow dominated the sky.

'I can give you my shares, though, and that's what I've done. The whole of my holdings in Kendal and Hunt are assigned to you—permanently. It's all quite legal. They're yours now. Joel has his, and when you finally get yours you'll own almost all of the firm. Right at this moment, however, you're the major shareholder—the one with all the power.'

She didn't know what to say, everything she had always thought now blurred.

'I don't need Kendal and Hunt,' he assured her, without even turning round. 'I've not needed it for a long time now. In any case, whether you marry me or not, the position remains the same. You now have control of the firm.'

'I don't want it!' She dropped the papers on the bed as if they were hot. 'I won't accept. You can't thrust this on me without my permission.'

'I'm not thrusting anything on you, Victoria.' He turned and looked at her, his face tightly controlled. 'I'm telling you that you are not in any way compelled to marry me.'

Cold fear raced through her. He was not at all upset. In spite of his vows to follow her to hell, he was coldly giving her freedom.

'You don't want to marry me after all?' She heard the numbness in her own voice, and it seemed to stiffen him even further.

'If what happened between us at the cottage is bothering you, then don't let it,' he said in an unyielding voice. 'We live in modern times, after all.' She flinched, but he went on relentlessly. 'As to this—feeling between us, I know you'll recover from it.'

'As readily as you have?' she whispered.

'I hope to hell not!' He gave a harsh laugh with no humour in it, his face once more turned to the black night and the red glow of Kendal and Hunt. 'I may seem cruel to you, but I'm not that cruel.'

He turned to look at her, and she felt he was forcing himself to face her, as if it needed courage.

'I've wanted you for longer than I care to remember,' he admitted bleakly. 'A feeling so strong seems to be enough. Now though, now that you're here, now that I see you with Joel, laughing, relaxed, happy to be with him, I realise that it's not enough. Perhaps I'm greedy, or maybe at last I can see into your mind and understand what this valley means to you. Andrew loved you, spoiled you in some things, but I know about the suppression too. He was of another age—maybe I am. You and Joel are closer than you and I will ever be, and I don't think I could take that. I don't see either why you should.'

'Joel—Joel is like a brother, I could never——'

'I'm not suggesting that you marry him, Victoria!' His hands clenched tightly beside him. 'I can't think of a worse nightmare than wanting to make love to my brother's wife!' He moved towards the door, not looking at her at all. 'I had the idea to give you those deeds on our wedding night. I've been rushing to get them prepared. It would be too late then, though. You wouldn't have any kind of choice.'

'I don't *want* them!' The vibrancy of her voice stopped him, and she picked up the papers and tore them in two. 'You can say you don't want to marry me without any kind of gesture, Damien! Just say it outright. You changed your mind. People do it all the time.'

She spun away from the intensity of his eyes, her head bent, her whole body tightly holding in grief.

'I—I never realised that Grandfather had you trapped too.' She gave a strange little laugh. 'To me, you were always the most powerful man in the world. I suppose I grew up under the shadow of that, terrified to offend you, fighting every step of the way rather than admit it. Grandfather manoeuvred me so easily. How did he manage it with you? I always thought he offered you the mills. Now you're giving everything to me. I don't understand any more.'

Her voice faded to a whisper, and Damien's voice was low.

'I wanted to marry you when you were eighteen. You ran away, made a new life. Andrew didn't manoeuvre you into that. You wanted to go. If I hadn't come to fetch you, you would never have seen this valley again. You never saw Andrew again!'

'I saw him all the time!' She turned to him wildly, her eyes filled with tears. 'We wrote to each other every week. He came to stay with me at least twice a year. We—we had a g-great time going out, seeing shows, we——'

'He never told me!'

Damien's voice was like ice, his eyes coldly blue, and her head fell beneath the threatening stare.

'I asked him not to, and obviously he kept his word— it would have appealed to his odd sense of humour.'

'Yes.' Damien's voice was a hollow sound. 'He let me find you and then took it from there. He never suffered as I thought. I was the one chosen to suffer. Your choice, Victoria!'

'Oh, you weren't the only one to suffer!' she said bitterly. 'I got mine in one great blow! Grandfather told me how he'd prepared me for you: my careful upbringing, my private school, my *cellophane* wrapping!

All for Damien Hunt! He was so pleased with his plans. He told me that you'd wanted me for years, and that everything had worked out nicely. When you married me, you would have the mills. You were quite ready to marry me, he said. I knew then why you'd swept me off my feet. The emerald pendant, the roses, the passion! It was so unlike you. I understood then, though. You both had to act fast before I found out, or before I looked for someone else!'

'He *told* you?'

'I've known since I was eighteen. So you see, I wasn't really surprised when you came for me after he died. The will shook me a little. I never expected him to have the cheek to put it all down in black and white!'

'And now?' He was beside her, turning her, his hands tightly on her shoulders. 'What do you believe now?'

'I don't know.' She shook her head, refusing to look up at him. 'I don't know what to believe any more.'

'We both know a little more than we did,' he said quietly, his fingers biting into her. 'Now you've told me what Andrew said to you, I understand why you ran away. Would you have run if he had never told you?'

'Oh, no!' She was startled into looking up. 'I used to dream that——' His hand caught her chin, keeping her gaze locked with his.

'I used to dream too,' he told her softly. 'I used to dream that the most beautiful girl in the world would be my wife one day. It was a dream that kept me waiting for her, and I was prepared to wait until she grew up, until she came to me. I was prepared to wait for a long time. When you were eighteen I bought the pendant and the ring you've got on your finger now, but I wasn't going to give you the ring. You weren't nearly ready.'

He looked down at her, his grip lessening, his hand stroking her face gently.

'When I came to your party, I went in to see Andrew first, and he was as excited as a child. He'd made his will that very morning. Everything to come to me until you married me, or until you were thirty.' He sighed and turned away, his hand leaving her with a gesture of hopelessness. 'For the first time in my life I wanted to hit an old man. I wanted to kill him! I didn't want the damned mills! The meeting was a wild row, because he just wouldn't listen. He was convinced you were utterly bewitched by me, that you would totally ignore any will just to be able to marry me. All I could get out of him was a promise that he would never tell you and, from the look in his eyes, I didn't place much faith in his promise. Andrew liked to have everyone know how well he planned. I had no time left.'

She was utterly silent, just staring at the raven dark of his hair as he let her go and turned away, and, as he suddenly turned back, the pain in his eyes was a shock that twisted at her heart.

'When I gave you the pendant, I almost told you then,' he confessed wearily. 'You looked so young, though, standing there with wide green eyes, not knowing at all what fate was planned for you. I couldn't do it. I wanted to take you with me and never come back, never let you find out and have black doubts about how I felt. I couldn't do that either, though. I loved you too much!'

'Loved me? Did you?' she asked weakly, tears in her eyes. 'Did you really love me then, Damien?'

'Always!' His hands came to her shoulders, his fingers softly caressing her neck, sliding inside the collar of her robe. 'That's why I can't ask you to marry me, not on the strength of any desire. It's not enough because, once again, I love you too much.'

The tears began to roll down her face as she looked at him wonderingly, hardly able to believe it.

'I wanted you to adore me,' she whispered. 'I wanted your face to light up with happiness when you saw me.'

'Didn't it?' he asked softly.

She looked at him, her heart suddenly beginning to soar. 'Yes. Later, though, I was so unhappy—I forgot. You never said you loved me, and I believed Grandfather instead of you. I love you, Damien! I never stopped. I——'

No further words were possible, because he caught her to him with such force that her breath almost stopped.

'Vicky! My beautiful love!' He held her away to look into her eyes, his expression wonderfully softened at the love he saw. 'I've wanted to tell you so often,' he murmured against her hair, drawing her back to him. 'I wanted to take you in my arms and let you know how I really felt, but I thought you hated me. Even so, I couldn't let you go; there had to be some hope that one day you wouldn't look at me with so much dislike.'

'I had to pretend,' she said urgently, her hand coming to his face. 'I had to fight for survival. I could never have faced a future without love.'

'You planned to, though,' he reminded her softly, his hand cupping her face.

'It was better than living without you,' she whispered, and he searched for her mouth gently.

'You'll never have to live without me. You're not allowed to cry,' he reminded her softly, as his lips covered hers.

The next morning Victoria was down very late. It was almost ten. The night before, she and Damien had talked until the sky had grown light, and she had slept in. Even so, when she went into the breakfast-room both Damien and Joel were still there.

'At last! Now we can get to work,' Joel remarked, as Damien came to kiss Victoria, and Molly bustled in with her breakfast.

'What are you doing here at this time?' Victoria asked in surprise.

'Damien wouldn't go until he'd seen you, and he wouldn't let anyone wake you up either!'

'Did that stop you from going?' Victoria asked wryly, her cheeks flushing as Damien simply sat and smiled at her.

'Naturally! I like to know what's going on,' Joel informed her, not one bit abashed.

'We're dining out tonight,' Damien murmured. 'I expect you'll want to be there too?'

'Ah! If I can bring a lady with me,' Joel said, with a quick grin at his brother. He got up resolutely. 'There'll be mayhem at the works. I've never known this sort of dallying from you, big brother.' He walked out, and Damien stood too, pausing by Victoria's chair to look down at her, his fingers caressing her cheek.

'What did you want to speak to me about?' she asked, looking up at him, still shy and in a dreamlike state.

'Nothing at all. I just wanted to see you, to assure myself that it was all real.' He bent and kissed her deeply. 'Do we let Joel come with us tonight?'

'I have to see this girl!' she laughed.

'Will you be jealous?' Damien asked, only partly joking.

'Only if you look at her twice,' Victoria looked up at him, and the blue eyes held hers.

'I'm not likely to do that,' he said deeply.

Even as they had dinner that night, there was a tightness about Damien. His eyes rarely left Victoria, and he had little to say to the other two, although Joel was the life and soul of the party. It was as well, Victoria thought—Joel needed to work hard to make up for the restraint that Damien showed, and that she was beginning to feel.

'What do you think of her?' Damien asked quietly as they danced.

'Not at all the sort of girl I would have imagined Joel with. In fact, I can't really bring to mind any sort of girl he would like.'

'Every sort!' Damien looked down at her as she gasped in surprise.

'Joel? He's a ladies' man?'

'Something of a sex symbol in these parts.'

'Then I don't know my old playmate too well either,' Victoria quipped.

'Don't remind me of the things I've said to you!' Damien muttered fiercely, pulling her close. He suddenly sighed wearily. 'Let's go home, Victoria.'

It was not the happy outing she had hoped for, but then, she and Damien were still like strangers. The drive home was almost silent and, when she went to bed, Joel had still not come in. She would have liked to be with Damien for longer, would have liked it if he was not able to do without her company—obviously he could.

Once again she was pacing her room, unable to sleep, her mind worrying over the way Damien was distant. Things were sorted out between them, but nothing was changed in one way—she would still be marrying a powerful stranger. Deep inside she knew that there was still a sense of distrust.

The lights were on in his room as she walked along the passage and, in spite of everything, it took a great deal of resolve to knock and open the door. He wasn't in bed. He was in a white bathrobe, and he, too, seemed to have been simply pacing the floor. He looked at her almost warily.

'I have to talk to you, Damien!' She closed the door and leaned against it determinedly.

'Is now a good time?' he asked quietly.

'I—I can't sleep. I need to talk to you.'

'All right.' He just stood and looked at her, watching her intently and, faced with it, she now didn't know what to say.

'We're not close!' She burst out with the words, and was rewarded by a quizzical look that had her cheeks flushing softly.

'You're in my bedroom. You want to be closer?'

It was no use. She couldn't speak to him reasonably. She never would be able to.

'I'll go. I'm sorry I——'

As she turned to leave he moved swiftly, his hands capturing her before she could even begin to open the door.

'You want to talk? I don't! I didn't want to sit and talk last night,' he said vibrantly. 'I wanted to make love to you. That's what I want to do now.'

His grasp on her shoulders was almost cruel, and she stared at him wildly.

'You—you never come near me! Since the other night you—— '

'You want me near you?' he asked almost violently, his grip biting into her. 'I hurt you! I've loved you for so long, so many damned frustrating years, and when you came to me I behaved like a savage.'

'Y-you didn't know. I let you believe——'

'And I believed it! In spite of the evidence of my eyes, in spite of your lovely, fastidious face, I believed it!'

'I made you believe it, Damien.'

'No! It was because I was jealous, desperate. I'm jealous now. I'm jealous of the ease with which you talk to Joel, the memories you share. I wanted you to see him with someone else, to realise that he's just a normal rogue, nothing special.'

'He'll always be special to me,' Victoria said softly. 'He looks a little like you. When the wind's in the right direction, he even sounds a little like you.' She smiled into his eyes, all the tension leaving her, and his expression softened, his grip easing to a caress.

'I'm hurting you now,' he murmured ruefully, his hands beginning to soothe her shoulders.

'Just so long as you're holding me,' she whispered.

'I daren't touch you!'

His hand caught her face, and her eyes closed at the passion she saw there, the shaken sound of his voice telling her how much he loved her.

'Then I'm always going to be hurt. I've waited too. I never stopped waiting, never stopped thinking about you. I've wanted you to love me for so long!'

'My lovely Victoria!' The strongest arms in the world lifted her to the bed and then closed around her as she opened her eyes and was drowned by the wonderful blue of his.

'Oh, Damien!' She wrapped her arms around his neck, arching towards him as his body hardened against her, his heart thudding against her own.

'You wanted to talk to me?' he breathed against her skin. He shrugged out of his robe and she responded feverishly to his every movement, nuzzling against his shoulder, her body taking on the exciting rhythm of his.

'Not now!' The wild plea in her voice brought his hand to the warmth of her thigh, and she felt the tension in him shatter as his hands slid her robe and nightie away, before moving beneath her, lifting her towards him.

'Darling! If I hurt you——'

'You called me "darling"!' she murmured, her eyes dazed with happiness. 'You—you said that——'

'That when somebody called you that and really meant it, you wouldn't know what had hit you,' he finished for her, gathering her even closer. 'I mean it. You've always been my darling. I've always loved you!'

He moved against her, unable to wait, his possession powerful, but so tender, and it was only her wild response to him that forced his constantly burning passion for her into the fierce clasp of his arms, the deep endless force of his kiss. The harshly murmured words of love were breathed against her lips, and she sobbed her own love-words against his mouth as he lifted her out of the world.

'I love you so much!' His skin was hot and damp as he buried his head against her, when the room had at last come back into her view. 'Don't leave me, darling. Stay here with me.'

'I was frightened you'd ask me to go away,' she laughed shakily.

'I never have asked you to go away!'

He raised his head and looked down at her, his hand smoothing the damp fair hair from her face and then tucking it behind her ears, as he suddenly smiled at her.

'Little habits from the past,' he murmured. 'Little things I loved, watched for, treasured.'

'You once called me a brat!' Victoria reminded him, her eyes mocking him.

'A beautiful brat, green-eyes,' he corrected, his lips brushing hers. 'It was a long time ago. Do you intend to hold that against me forever?'

'It hurt me!' she protested, her fingers trailing down his well-loved face. 'I took a long time to recover.'

'Then you didn't hear the end of the conversation, did you?' he mocked. 'I asked why we didn't install you there permanently, and my mother said that she'd like to.'

'Did she really?' Victoria asked, her smile pleased and happily reminiscent. 'I was always glad to be with her.'

'She never had a girl. You were the only girl in the two families for as far back as anyone could remember. You were something of a miracle. She would have liked to add you to the household—I felt just the same. That's what I told her.'

He kissed her gently, but she pulled away, looking up at him.

'Damien, I—I want to know about Heather.'

'There's nothing to know about Heather,' he murmured, punctuating his answer with swift kisses. 'I took her on as a secretary because she was good at the job.'

'She said that you...anyway, you took her out!' Victoria said, staring up at him with annoyance.

'Only to make you think there was more in my life than a green-eyed, beautiful witch,' he grinned. 'Have I ever in the past shown any sign of being anything other than irritated by Heather?' He smiled down at her when she shook her head a little worriedly. 'I don't mind you being jealous,' he said softly, 'but you've got to feel safe. I've loved you since you were about sixteen, maybe even before that. There hasn't been much room in my life for anyone else. They all tended to look like you if I closed my eyes. The older you got, the more explosive the feeling became. It got to the stage when I couldn't exist without you.'

Victoria looked up at him wistfully, and he smiled into her eyes. 'Then Grandfather upset everything,' she said softly.

'Yes! The old devil!' Damien moved to the side, his arms around her waist, his eyes turning back to her with startled appraisal as she began to laugh softly.

'What's so funny?' he asked fiercely. 'I lost you for years!'

'But you've found me again,' she told him gently, lifting herself to look down into his face. 'Perhaps it was as well. I would never have been a match for you.'

'You think you are now?' He grinned up at her and her heart lifted at the happiness on his face.

'Now I know your weak spot!' she said slyly.

'And what's that?' His hand cupped her face gently, as he pulled her slowly towards him.

'Me!' she whispered against his lips.

'Ah! You've found out.' He enfolded her in his arms, his lips searching her skin with growing desire, but she pulled away a little and looked at him seriously.

'Damien, can I have my pendant back?' she said softly.

The blue eyes opened wide and he watched her intently, before his arm reached out to the drawer of the bedside table, the golden chain in his hand as he turned back to her.

'You have to lie in my arms and beg,' he said huskily. 'I always carry out my threats.'

'Please, darling,' she pleaded against his smiling mouth, and he slid it over her head, his eyes following the progress of the glittering emerald as it moved to the shadowy hollow between her breasts.

'Is it a bond of slavery?' he asked softly, his eyes gloriously blue and filled with desire.

'No. It's a token of love,' she whispered, 'and I've never given you anything at all.'

'Oh, Vicky!' he murmured against her lips. 'You've given me my whole life, my every happiness, my past and my future.'

He drew back to look at her, his face alight, adoration in his eyes, and her heart began to beat wildly.

'I love you, Damien,' she said. 'I told you a long time ago, and I've never stopped meaning it.'

His lips closed over hers, and she sank into the happiness of the destiny that had waited for her for so long.

HARLEQUIN

Coming Next Month

#3103 TO TAME A COWBOY Katherine Arthur
Jennifer needed to get away from the city, her parents' bickering and a violent
boyfriend. A ranch in Montana seems far enough, her new boss Clay Cooper a warm
generous man. Jennifer begins to relax until she finds herself an unwilling
participant in another family's row!

#3104 CITY GIRL, COUNTRY GIRL Amanda Clark
Stung by a bee, knocked down by a huge muddy dog—that's Hannah's introduction
to country life. So the last thing she expects is to actually *enjoy* the enforced
vacation. Or to fall in love with a country vet named Jake McCabe....

#3105 THE GIRL WITH GREEN EYES Betty Neels
When Lucy meets eminent pediatrician William Thurloe, she determines to become
the woman of his dreams. The fact she is neither clever nor sophisticated like Fiona
Seymour, who wants William, too, is just one small obstacle she has to overcome.

#3106 OF RASCALS AND RAINBOWS Marcella Thompson
Kristy Cunningham races to Mount Ida, Arkansas, to find her missing grandfather.
She runs up against her granddad's young partner and self-proclaimed protector—
and the strangest feeling that she must stay, no matter what....

#3107 THE GOLDEN THIEF Kate Walker
Leigh Benedict seems to think every young aspiring actress is a pushover for the
casting couch, and his cynical attitude appalls Jassy. But the attraction that flows
between them makes it difficult for her to convince him otherwise.

#3108 THAI SILK Anne Weale
Clary helps a fellow Briton in trouble in Thailand by summoning Alistair Lincoln
halfway around the world to bail out his stepsister. But when he insists on Clary
sharing responsiblity for young Nina, it's Alistair who becomes the problem.

**Available in February wherever paperback books are sold, or through
Harlequin Reader Service:**

In the U.S.
901 Fuhrmann Blvd.
P.O. Box 1397
Buffalo, N.Y. 14240-1397

In Canada
P.O. Box 603
Fort Erie, Ontario
L2A 5X3